WATERSHED

Chris Crowther

Other books by Chris Crowther

The *Jack Fellows* Series:
WATERPROOF
STILL WATERS
THE WATER FROLIC
WATER UNDER THE BRIDGE
MURKY WATERS
DEAD IN THE WATER

Younger reading:
TIMECRUISER

Published in the U.S:
BLADESTRIKE

British Library Cataloguing in Publication Data
A catalogue record is available from the British Library.

ISBN 978-1-9998111-1-2

First published this edition in 2021

by

TALEWEAVER • HOVETON • NORFOLK NR12 8UJ

WWW.CHRISCROWTHER.CO.UK

PRINTED IN GREAT BRITAIN BY BARNWELL PRINT LTD
DUNKIRK • AYLSHAM • NORFOLK NR11 6SU
WWW.BARNWELLPRINT.CO.UK

ILLUSTRATIONS BY SARAH ROGERS

Chris Crowther

Taleweaver

Dear Reader,

This book, one of my seven "Jack Fellows" murder-mysteries set on the Norfolk Broads, is yours to take home and keep. If you'd like any of the others, including WATERSHED, which came out just this year, or TIMECRUISER, my children's fantasy adventure, they can be obtained from local shops or direct through my website shown below. I'd love to hear from you. In the meantime, I wish you a great Broadland holiday.

Sincerely

Chris

Email: taleweaver@chriscrowther.co.uk   Website: www.chriscrowther.co.uk

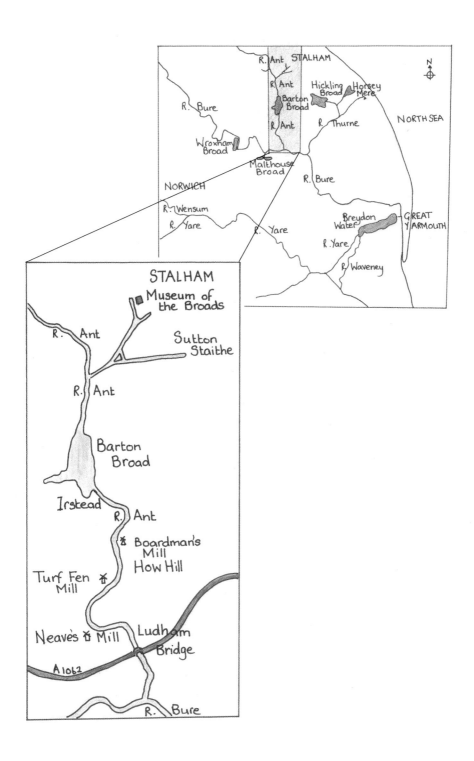

Yesterday, upon the stair
  I met a man who wasn't there.
He wasn't there again today.
  Oh how I wish he'd go away

William Hughes Mearns
(1875-1965)

Chapter One

'Fancy a trip on a steamboat, Aud?'

Jack Fellows came back into the kitchen from answering the hall phone with a wide grin on his face. Audrey looked up from her mid-morning coffee. Outside she could see spring sunshine already glinting through the cherry blossom trees. 'Sounds lovely, Jack. I presume it has something to do with this weekend's steamboat rally?'

'Yep. That was Laura Lampeter, *Steambuffs'* secretary. She arrived last night from up north and wants to meet us at the Museum of the Broads.'

'That's where their rally's starting off, isn't it?'

'On Saturday, yes, but she'd like us there in forty-five minutes.'

'Right, we'd better get our skates on then,' said Audrey, scooping up their coffee cups and stashing them into the sink. 'And, while we're getting ready, you can tell me again just what your role is in all this?'

'Just keeping an eye on things really. There'll be a lot of folk out on the river just to see their classic boats, so the Broads Authority has designated me to act as escort.'

Audrey gave a wry smile. 'Well, being a bit of a steam buff yourself, they couldn't have chosen a more enthusiastic ranger. But today's only Wednesday and you said they don't start arriving until Friday, so why this meeting?'

'Because Laura's booked us on *Falcon* as a taster.'

'The museum steamboat ... well, I bet she didn't have to suggest that twice. You've been itching for a trip on that boat for years and never got round to it. What time are we sailing?'

'Eleven-thirty, so we need to get moving.' Sensing an imminent outing, Spike, the Fellows' faithful border collie emerged from beneath the kitchen table, tail wagging and a face full of anticipation. Jack gave the old dog an encouraging pat. 'Yes, old chap, they said you can come too, just as long as you behave yourself.'

'This'll certainly be a more interesting morning than the one I had planned,' said Audrey as, ten minutes later, all three climbed in the car.

'Perhaps in more ways than one, Aud, because I got the impression Laura had some other agenda she wanted to discuss.' Jack glanced at the dashboard clock. 'Anyway, not long now and we'll find out.'

*   *   *

Jack had never met Laura Lampeter, but over their few phone calls he'd formed a mental image that came close to the tall, casually dressed slim figure with shoulder length auburn hair, standing on the museum staithe. She was so intent on watching *Falcon* getting up steam that she didn't even notice the Fellows' arrival until they were by her side.

'Great, isn't she?' said Jack, joining her in admiration of this twenty-seven foot, lovingly restored teak launch.

She spun around, her look of concentration breaking into a ready smile. 'Ah ... Jack ... good to put a face to the voice on the phone. And you must be Audrey,' she said, shaking hands before turning back to *Falcon*. 'And, yes, a lovely old boat. I can't wait to see her in action.'

'Nor me.'

That time would not be long coming because already two elderly passengers were cautiously stepping into the open bow area ahead of the machinery space, leaving Jack and company to the open stern cockpit with the skipper.

'What lovely weather,' said Audrey, settling down onto one of the side seats while breathing in spring air and the whiff of coal smoke spiralling from *Falcon*'s shining brass funnel, 'and the perfect way to enjoy it.' With Spike sitting obediently at her feet, his head resting on her knee, she briefly closed her eyes and gave a contented sigh.

But it was the boat's machinery amidships, with its gleaming fittings and white-lagged pipe work that had got Jack's attention. 'A compound, isn't it?'

Laura nodded. 'That's right, and double acting in that the steam pressure drives both pistons both ways.' She caught Audrey's blank look. 'Sorry, Audrey, that means the engine is very efficient ... as we're about to find out,' she added, as the skipper signalled the shore party to cast off the lines before a short hoot on the steam whistle and a burst of prop wash had them easing away from the quay.

'This is how a boat should sound,' said Jack, as the rhythmic hiss of well-oiled pistons and the sluice of water down the hull's gleaming black sides provided the only accompaniment to their smooth passage down the dyke. 'Wonderful.'

'Yes, and so effortless too.' Laura gave a wistful shake of her head. 'Why is it that old boats seem to want to go faster?'

The skipper nodded in agreement. 'We have to hold her back. She'll do ten

2

knots if we really open her up.'

For now though the crew were content to merely up the revs slightly as *Falcon* cleared the museum dyke and headed downstream at the permitted 4mph. Enforcing these limits to protect the fragile river banks from erosion was part of Jack's job as a ranger and one that would be a lot easier if all boats cut through the water as cleanly as *Falcon*. Even Audrey was impressed. 'She's so much quieter than I expected.'

'That's steam power for you.' Laura tilted her head back and breathed in the slight southerly breeze that, together with the boat's own forward speed, was sufficient to stream out the pennant at the masthead and leave their funnel smoke trailing blissfully astern. As they came abeam a small cut leading off to the left, Laura checked their position on the map she'd just pulled from her rucksack. 'That must lead to Sutton Staithe.'

Jack nodded. 'The staithe is only a short way along what used to be Sutton Broad until the reeds reduced it to just the width of a dyke.'

'Well, that's our first port of call on Saturday,' pointed out Laura, stowing away her map. 'We're at the museum all day for visitors to see our gathering of launches, and then in the evening we're off to Sutton for a social get-together in the hotel.' She leant across to give Spike's head a stroke and raised questioning eyebrows to the Fellows. 'I hope both of you can join us for that.'

Jack glanced at Audrey, who nodded enthusiastically. 'Thanks very much for the invite. We'd love to.'

'Great. It'll give you a chance to get to know everyone.'

As they continued downriver, the waterway became busier with passing traffic on its way to Stalham, mostly hire cruisers heading back to the boatyard, their crews both surprised and excited to see *Falcon* steaming gracefully by. Enthusiastic waves were returned with a cheerful toot on the steam whistle and friendly smiles from those onboard. Audrey cast a glance at the look of pleasure on Jack's face. 'Enjoying it, love?'

'Absolutely.' He gave the teak hull a loving slap. 'My idea of heaven, Aud.'

'And mine too,' joined in Laura. 'What could be more perfect than cruising down a Broadland river in a Victorian steamboat with the sun shining?'

'Actually, we're not on the main river yet,' explained the skipper, giving the brass tiller a slight input to ease them around the next bend, 'but we soon will be. That's the River Ant, straight ahead.'

'It doesn't look very different to the waterway we're already on,' said Laura, turning from watching the engineer shovel another load of coal into the firebox.

'You're right, it all seems natural now, but these dykes were dug by man seven-hundred years ago, whereas that river has been here as long as the world.'

They were soon on it, following its course downstream towards Barton around natural meanders, overshadowed now by alder trees instead of the open reedbeds that had lined the dykes. In secluded spots, cruisers lay moored to the bank by single-fluked spikes. 'On the Broads, the river bank is called "the rhond",' explained Jack, 'so those mooring hooks are called "rhond-anchors".'

'I can see there are a few locally used words I need to get used to,' said Laura with a smile, noticing the moored craft hardly moving in *Falcon*'s modest wash and with only the nostalgic tang of smoke hanging briefly in the air to mark the steamboat's passing. She glanced again at her map. 'I presume that's Barton Broad ahead?'

Sure enough, a huge expanse of open water was coming into view. Soon *Falcon*'s straight stem was cleaving its glistening surface as the engineer increased speed and the launch's curling bow wave joined the small wavelets advancing up the broad.

'This is the second largest broad and the only one with river flowing through it,' explained Jack. He pointed to the exit at the far end. 'And that's where the Ant continues its way south, flowing for another four and a half miles past Irstead and Ludham before it joins the River Bure.'

'Ah, we'll be exploring that stretch of river on Sunday, but I'll explain the full plan later,' said Laura, looking up from her map in time to see a sailing cruiser crossing their bows as it tacked in the freshening breeze. 'This is such a beautiful place ... I'm surprised I never came here.'

Jack nodded. 'Up until quite recently, no-one could unless they had a boat. Now, though, there's a boardwalk linking it to the village of Neatishead and a viewing platform overlooking the entire broad.' He paused as he realised the full significance of Laura's words. 'But it sounds as if you've been to Norfolk before.'

'Yes, I lived in Norwich for three years when I was a student at the UEA.'

'You were at the University of East Anglia?' said Audrey, surprised. 'How long ago was that?'

'Over twelve years now.' Just for a second, Laura's mouth dropped slightly. 'My goodness, where did they go? So much has happened since then.'

Audrey couldn't help feeling there was a note of sadness in that last statement, but now wasn't the time to spoil such a lovely time afloat with probing questions. Perhaps she'd learn more later. For the moment she settled down to enjoy the rest of the trip.

'I don't know about you two, but I'm ready for this,' said Jack, gently lowering three coffees onto the small table and taking a seat.

They were in the museum's café area, Spike eagerly lapping water from the bowl kindly provided by the shop staff and Laura looking around her at the large models of Norfolk wherries surrounding them, including a full-scale replica of a wherry cabin. Just outside was another display area brimming with boats of every description, their gear and the means by which they worked in Broadland's old trading days. 'This is great,' she enthused before turning back to her coffee. 'Everyone in *Steambuffs* has an interest in nautical history, so this is the perfect place to start the rally.'

'Are there many of you coming?' asked Audrey.

'Five boats, including three already based here on the Broads,' she explained between sips of coffee. 'The other two, including our *Osprey*, are being trailered down from up north. We have a rally at a different place each year and this time, thanks to Dexter, we chose the Broads.'

'Dexter?' queried Jack.

'Yes, Dexter Berrington, one of our local owners. He and his wife Margo run an art gallery in Norwich, but he moors *Pickle* close to here.'

'Yes, I know that boat,' recalled Jack. 'A lovely little regatta launch, but I've yet to meet the owner.'

'He's ex-Merchant Navy,' said Laura, 'so you'll like him.'

'I'm sure I will.' Jack took out a pocket notebook and clicked his pen. 'So, what's the programme for the weekend?'

'We'll be spending Saturday here at the museum for a public Steamboat Day, then move on to Sutton afterwards for our dinner at the Staithe Hotel and overnight mooring. Next morning ...' she paused to pull out her map and pointed to a spot halfway down the Ant, 'we're off to here ... How Hill.'

'Good choice,' concurred Jack. 'Plenty of moorings, and the house has one of the finest views in Broadland.'

'And beautiful walks and gardens,' added Audrey.

'Well, there'll be even more attractions on Sunday,' said Laura, 'because they're making it a steam themed day there as well. Apart from our boats, Lionel Hillbeck will be displaying his traction engine and giving sawing demonstrations. He and his wife are *Steambuffs* members and own *Whisper*, a lovely old launch.'

'But your boat is *Osprey*,' recalled Audrey.

'I wish,' lamented Laura, 'but, at forty-two feet and fourteen tons, she's more boat than I could ever afford to run. She's actually been in the family for generations, but now Father has nominal ownership ...' she gave an impish grin, '... so he pays the bills and I just have all the fun skippering her.'

'Nice for you,' said Jack, 'but doesn't your father want to get hands-on at all?'

She gave a good chuckle. 'Good Lord no. He's got no interest in boats other than for entertaining. Besides, he always reckoned he never had time when he was running RLC.'

'RLC?'

'*Ralph Lampeter Construction*, the family business ... or *was*, until it went bust along with my parents' marriage just after I finished uni.'

'That must have been a difficult time for you,' sympathised Audrey.

'Yes, but life goes on, and since they split up, Father's been quite happy for me to skipper *Osprey*.'

'On your own?'

'Not quite, Audrey. Jim Rowston, the engineer who carried out *Osprey*'s refit, comes along to look after the technical side.'

'Will he be at the rally?'

'Oh yes. He has his own berth on board.'

'And you sleep on the boat as well?'

'Yep, but it's not what you think, Audrey,' assured Laura with a smile. 'Having had my fingers burned once, I've no intention of going down that road again. But Jim's a good engineer who came to us through *New Start*.'

'*New Start*?'

'Yes, that's the charity my father started up after RLC's demise. It helps ex-prisoners get back into useful work. Father always took on one or two when his business was doing well, believing that regular employment would give them a fresh start and stop them reoffending.'

'What a good cause,' applauded Audrey. 'Your dad sounds a lovely man and I look forward to meeting him.'

'Except I'm afraid you won't,' said Laura with a disparaging sniff, 'because he's not coming. Reckons he's busier than ever now with *New Start*.'

Jack frowned. 'Hardly seems worth his while then to own a big boat like *Osprey*?'

'He won't for much longer,' said Laura with a catch in her voice, 'because he's selling her.'

'I can see you're not happy with that.'

'No, and neither is Mum. We've tried to talk him out of it, but now he's using the excuse of his heart condition.'

'Not a serious one, I hope?' Audrey looked concerned.

'No, pretty mild actually and easily controlled with herbal medication, but he's intent on selling dear old *Osprey*, so she's probably going to Dexter Berrington.'

'For his private use?' asked Jack.

But Laura shook her head. 'No, Dexter's got some plan to run her as a trip boat here on the Broads. Father would probably have come this weekend, if only to close the deal. I suspect the *real* reason he's not is that my mum *will be*.'

'So, your mother must be Helen Lampeter,' said Jack. 'I remember she applied for a temporary toll for the steamboat *Sunbeam* ... registered jointly by her and a Charles Seager.'

'Mum's partner,' explained Laura. 'Charles was RLC's legal officer until he became the third side of the triangle.'

Audrey nodded understanding. 'Yes, I can see now why your father's keeping well clear of the rally, but I'm sure you'll be glad to see your mum again.'

'Yes ... and Charles. He's good for Mum and he helped me when ...' then she stopped and shrugged away what seemed sad memories, '... but lots to do here and now, including another thing I was hoping you might help me with, Jack.'

'Which is?'

'Something still to do with steamboats, but going back a couple of centuries.' She finished her coffee. 'You see, part of my running *Steambuffs* includes editing their magazine, which fits in quite nicely with my job as a freelance journalist. What I'd like to do while I'm here is research an article on the loss of the *Telegraph*.'

'A paddle steamer, wasn't she? Didn't she blow up in Norwich in ... ?'

'... 1817,' completed Laura. 'I researched the disaster as a writing project when I was at uni, but never took it any further. Now seems a good time to get some pictures and delve a little further into the story, including visiting the Great Hospital, where I understand the badly injured were taken. Would that be possible?'

'It's still there, but as sheltered accommodation now. A lovely place though with a fascinating history.'

'And where one of our old parishioners now lives,' added Audrey, 'so we do know a few of the staff there.' She brightened with an idea. 'Look, Jack's off for the next couple of days and we're going into Norwich ourselves tomorrow to

7

do a bit of shopping. I'll call someone to check it's okay and, if it is, why don't you two meet up for a wander round the grounds?'

'That would be super,' said Laura, gratefully. '*Osprey* arrives the next day and I'll be busy with her after that, so tomorrow's perfect.'

'All being well, how about we meet at Foundry Bridge at ten-thirty?' suggested Jack, quite content to be missing a spot of shopping. 'That's just about where *Telegraph* had her explosion and then we could walk to the hospital beside the river.'

'Talking of walks,' interrupted Audrey, 'Spike's getting bit restless. I think he's ready for his.'

'Of course,' said Laura, standing up. 'Send me a text just to confirm it's all okay ... but can I push my luck and ask one more favour?'

Jack smiled as he stood up himself. 'Go ahead.'

'Well, we'll be craning *Osprey* into the water on Friday. Any chance of you joining us for that?'

'I'd love to.'

'Great, and you'll get to meet Dexter. He wants to see the boat again before committing himself.'

'Not running the art gallery that day then?'

'Not if he can get his wife to cover for him. Margo bought *ArtVu* soon after we finished our degrees, but she's seldom there these days and just leaves poor Dexter to hold the fort.'

'So, were you and Margo old college friends then?' asked Audrey.

'We *were*,' said Laura, picking up her rucksack. 'But nothing is forever.'

*　　*　　*

ArtVu, Margo Berrington's single fronted gallery, was situated in one of Norwich's narrow, rambling backstreets and this day, like most, lacking both its owner and customers. Instead, it was in the hands of her husband whose only interest in paintings were seascapes, and then only to remind himself of a life now as seemingly distant as the sea itself.

Well-built with dark close-cropped hair, Dexter was still trying to come to terms with his role as assistant. Margo had indeed owned this gallery long before they met and married and, besotted as he was with a girl as vivacious as she was single-minded, he'd willingly sacrificed both career and prospects on the altar of pure passion. Never one to break a promise, he had tried to adapt, but once the honeymoon period had worn off and the harsh reality of a boring passionless life with Margo had struck home, bitterness began eating into him. With a marriage now as meaningless as his life, the only bright spot had been *Pickle*.

Buying and running that old steamboat had at least kept a sliver of maritime lore running through his veins and an escape from the tedium of *ArtVu*. But then had come the possibility of permanent escape with word that Ralph Lampeter was considering selling *Osprey*, a boat perfect in size and character for running a traditional steamboat service out of Norwich. Having done his sums, and against fierce opposition from Margo, he'd made an offer and been told it would be considered.

It would be a tight budget, but manageable by selling *Pickle*. In fact, he already had another member interested in buying her. Harry Bryant's small engineering business had already made some replacement engine parts for the boat and, although he wasn't a character Dexter would have chosen to sell his beloved *Pickle* to, it was at least a way to making his own dream come true.

He would have liked to enjoy that dream a bit longer on this monotonous morning, but it was suddenly cut short by the jangle of *ArtVu*'s doorbell. He looked up to see wife Margo elbowing her shapely figure inside, overnight case in one hand and some designer-label carrier bags in the other.

'Oh, it's you.' Knowing that it was only his wife's other mysterious dealing that kept the gallery financially afloat, Dexter bit his tongue as she dumped her shopping and case behind the counter. 'You're back early. I didn't expect you for another day.'

'Or any customers either, by the look of it. Not exactly crowded, is it?'

'It never is.' One issue they did at least agree on was that *ArtVu*'s accounts were as depressing as the gallery itself. 'I don't know why you stick with this place. You own the freehold, so why not just sell up and concentrate on your other business. Obviously, that and your secret trips away are much more lucrative.'

Margo rolled her eyes. 'You'd love me to sell this place, wouldn't you? Then you could just sit back and let me bankroll this ludicrous boat business you keep harping on about.'

'I wouldn't be asking *you* for anything, Margo. Buying *Osprey* would mean I was investing *my* time and *my* money into a business *I'd* actually enjoy.'

'What, running jollies down the river? Do me a favour.' Margo shook her head, despairingly. 'You realise, of course, that you'll never see a return on your ...' she made little quotations with her fingers, '... "investment"?'

'Maybe not, but at least I'll be doing something I love.'

'Oh, really?' Margo was making no effort to disguise the contempt in her voice. 'Well, at least that way you'd love *something*.'

'I'm not doing this just for *me*, Margo. I know I seem to have lost the spark for anything these days, but that's just a consequence of my general unhappiness with all this.' He waved his hand over the gallery's displays of garish oil paintings and mediocre watercolours. 'If only you'd start painting again, we'd have something decent to sell. You haven't picked up a brush since we've been married and that landscape,' he pointed to the large watercolour on display in the gallery window, 'is the only one of yours we have left to offer.'

'And that wouldn't be on show now if you hadn't gone and dragged it down from the loft.' Margo glanced upwards. 'And you can put it back up there just as soon as I've unpacked. You're not the only discontented one, Dexter. I need to be happy to paint and I haven't been that for years.'

'Perhaps we'd both be happier doing something we enjoyed.' Dexter, edged closer to his wife and tentatively put his arm around her shoulders. 'If I started my boat business and you got painting again, we might put a bit of excitement back into our married life as well.'

But Margo shrugged him off. 'I doubt it. Right now, the only thing to put a bit of life back into me would be a stiff drink, so do the one thing you're good at and go and pour me one.'

Their home was a small flat above the gallery, and Dexter trudged up there now, wondering if he still possessed even an atom of self-respect. He'd once commanded men, but was now reduced to being nothing but a lap-dog. After putting the kettle on, he stood pondering just how long this marital state of affairs could endure. Perhaps buying *Osprey* would provide escape in more ways than one. He poured Margo's whisky, made his coffee and went back downstairs to find a scene drastically different from the one he'd left just minutes before.

His wife was still standing beside the counter, but now deathly white and seemingly frozen into immobility, her shocked gaze fixed on the gallery display window. She jumped as Dexter touched her shoulder.

'Good heavens, Margo, are you all right? What on earth's the matter?'

But Margo, never one to be normally short of words, now seemed to be struggling to find more than two as she pointed a shaking finger at the street outside. 'A man.'

'A man?' Dexter looked, but saw only pedestrians and shoppers obliviously scuttling by. 'What man? What did he do?'

Margo was starting to pull herself together. 'He ... he was staring ... staring at the painting.'

'At the landscape? What's wrong with that?' Dexter was beginning to wonder if his wife was losing it completely. 'He was probably just admiring it,

Margo ... perhaps even considering buying it.'

'No he wasn't. He was just looking at it ... sort of fixated.' She grabbed the whisky tumbler and took a full swig, bringing a swift return of colour to her cheeks and some of the old feistiness. 'It's all your fault. You had go and put that damned painting in the window didn't you?'

'That's what we do, Margo ... sell paintings.'

'Yes, well not that one, so take it out right now.'

Realising there was no point arguing, Dexter simply obeyed, removing the offending landscape and sticking it out of sight behind the counter. 'There, does that make you happier?' He didn't expect an answer, let alone any thanks, but his wife's next question seemed oddly out of context.

'This steamboat thing you're attending this weekend. Are you still going?'

'Yes, of course I am. Why?'

'Because I thought I might come too.'

'But you've *never* been to one of *Steambuffs'* rallies, Margo, and swore you never would.'

'Yes, well this weekend I'd rather not be alone, so count me in.'

And with that, Margo knocked back the remains of her whisky and disappeared upstairs, leaving her husband more baffled than ever.

*   *   *

Chapter Two

'Still half an hour before we need to get going,' said Jack, checking the kitchen clock. It was next morning in the Fellows' kitchen and, having already walked Spike, he was just finishing his cooked breakfast and looking forward to his meeting with Laura in the city. 'Thanks for checking with the Great Hospital, Aud. Good to know they're happy for me to show Laura around.'

'Especially as it gets you out of trailing around the shops with me,' said Audrey, enjoying a little dig as she fished two slices of bread out of the toaster and joined Jack at the table. 'Anyway, I think she'll enjoy your company. I got the impression she's a bit lonely here on her own.'

'Yes, strange isn't it that she hasn't arranged catch-ups with any of her old university pals while she's here. There must be a few living in the area.'

'She certainly didn't seem very keen to see that Margo Berrington again.' Audrey passed across the toast rack. 'I wonder what went wrong there?'

'Probably a boy,' grunted Jack, helping himself to butter and marmalade. 'It usually is.'

'Well, it had to be something quite serious if she's still harbouring bad feelings after twelve years.' Audrey pondered for a moment before coming to the same conclusion as her husband. 'I think you may be right about it being over a boy, because something certainly happened in the past to put Laura off men.'

'...which happens all the time, Aud. It's a hard fact of life, as we know only too well with our two.' Jack poured himself another coffee. 'But, whatever it was, it must have hit her hard, poor girl.'

'Perhaps it just happened at a vulnerable time for her, when everything was going wrong at home. Anyway, Jack, it's none of our business, though I'm sorry I won't be meeting her father at the weekend. He sounds like a good man, starting up such a worthwhile charity.'

'Hmm, I'm not so sure.'

'Why do you say that?'

'Just a gut feeling he might not be all he seems, love. I mean, his business went bust and yet he still has enough money to run a boat the size of *Osprey*.' Jack shrugged. 'It's probably the old story of a business folding and everyone losing out except the person who ran it. Ralph Lampeter no doubt gives the outward impression of being a do-gooder, but I bet he's getting *something* out of it.'

'Oh Jack, why do you have to be so cynical?' grumbled Audrey despairingly, while gathering up the breakfast things. 'You're not a Scotland Yard detective anymore, so don't go turning a charitable endeavour into something negative.' She shrugged. 'Okay, I did notice a lack of warmth in Laura's voice when she talked about her father, but that's probably only because she's closer to her mother.'

'What makes you think that?'

'It's simple. Didn't you notice that she always called her mother "Mum", but him, "Father"? That's a sure sign of how children view their parents.'

'Now who's being the detective?' chided Jack, while impressed by his wife's reasoning and trying to remember what their own daughters called him. 'Anyway, whatever Laura's parental loyalties, it's time we got going to Norwich if I'm to meet her on time.'

'You'll enjoy giving her a hand researching the *Telegraph* disaster, love.'

'Very much so ... but sorry it won't include you, Spike,' added Jack, seeing the collie's reproachful look at being left behind.

Spike might not be the only one disappointed by the time this week was over, thought Audrey as she went off to get herself ready. She wished the rally every success even though her husband's intuition already seemed to be working overtime. Perhaps he was right in thinking that not all was quite what it seemed.

*　　*　　*

'Hi, Jack.' Laura smiled and waved as the ranger joined her on Norwich's Foundry Bridge. 'Good to see you.'

'And you.' She hadn't been difficult to spot in her bright yellow sailing jacket, worn against the damp mist that had been hanging over the city since early morning and was only just beginning to lift. Jack glanced skyward to where patches of blue were already appearing. 'Great, the sun's starting to break through. It'll be a lovely walk to the Hospital. We'll take the riverside path, which is probably the route they took back then with *Telegraph*'s casualties.'

'Sounds perfect.' Laura turned away from the noisy mid-morning traffic and leaned over the bridge parapet. 'I always thought Norwich was such a wonderful mixture of ancient and modern.' She was looking down to the

Yacht Station where a few hire-cruisers lay moored along its quarter mile length while another was already passing beneath them, making the most of the ebb tide towards Great Yarmouth. 'I wonder if Good Friday in 1817 was like this?'

'Was that the day *Telegraph* blew up?'

'Yes. She was just setting off on her scheduled daily service to Yarmouth. It used to take her just over three and a half hours each way.'

'Crikey, so two centuries ago they were doing it faster than we do now!' exclaimed Jack. 'Of course, they weren't worried about bank erosion or speed limits in those days, so they could go flat out.'

'And, with no trains then, it was the fastest way to go,' emphasised Laura, 'but *Telegraph* wasn't the only boat running that service at the time. A chap called Thomas Watts was in competition with another steamer called *Nelson*. On the morning of the disaster, both boats were scheduled to leave this bridge together, so it was going to be a race from the start. As it was, *Telegraph* got away first but, within minutes, her boiler exploded.'

'Presumably caused by piling on too much steam?'

'Yes, and in a boiler ruined by salt water on a previous trip from the Medway, and repaired by bolting a new cast-iron end onto the old wrought-iron. That created a weak spot but, instead of taking it easy, the engineer had hung weights on the safety valve to push things to the limit.'

'With disastrous results.'

'Very. The paddle wheels had only made three turns when that cast-iron end shattered, the whole boiler broke loose and shot like a rocket through the transom.'

'It must have been mayhem,' said Jack, imagining the scene. 'How many were onboard?'

'Twenty-two. Nine were killed instantly and two more died later. Many of the others were scalded by high-pressure steam or seriously injured by flying debris. They were taken to the Great Hospital.'

'Which is where we'll soon be,' said Jack, leading them down the adjacent steps to the pathway following the river's inner bank. 'This used to be the boundary of the old city wall.'

'More history,' said Laura, obviously in her element. 'This is wonderful.'

*　　*　　*

As Jack had promised, it was a pleasant walk along the footpath beside the River Wensum. By now the sun was filtering through the overhanging trees to glint enchantingly on the slightly dappled water. They'd just reached the ancient Watergate of Pulls Ferry and were pausing to admire the rising might of the Cathedral spire, when the ping of Laura's mobile reminded them they were still in the twenty-first century.

'Sorry, Jack ... a text,' she apologised before reading the message. Then, having made no attempt to reply, she impatiently switched off with an exasperated sigh.

'Not disappointing news, I hope?'

'Irritating more like. That was from a member called Harry Bryant. He's hoping to buy Dexter's *Pickle*, but already in Norwich and asking if we could meet for a meal.'

'Which you're obviously not keen to do?'

'I'm certainly not. He runs a small engineering outfit in the Midlands and has made a lot of parts for our steam engines, but he's constantly pestering me for a date. Unlike another I won't mention, I'm not desperate enough to go out with men twice my age, but I can't seem to get that across to Bryant.'

'How did he know you were already here in Norwich?'

'Probably my father told him.'

'They're friends?'

'Not as such, but he's an ex-offender, and the charity helped him set up his own engineering business. Now *Heritage Engineering* takes on chaps from *New Start*, so Father probably feels he owes him something.'

'But you don't?'

'Not until Hell freezes over, Jack.'

'Okay, but don't write off all men just because you've been hurt once.'

'I suppose you're right. Who knows what the future will bring.' Clearly ready to change the subject, she nodded towards the squat bulk of a church tower just beyond the Norwich School playing fields. 'What church is that?'

'Saint Helen's. It's part of the Great Hospital. We'll soon be there.'

'Brilliant.'

She set off again, still apparently enthusiastic, though giving Jack the feeling that her thoughts were tending to stray elsewhere. Perhaps that text from Harry Bryant had upset her more than he thought.

*   *   *

Less than a quarter mile away and sprawled on his hotel room bed, the man himself shifted just sufficiently to check again the mobile phone lying close by. Still no reply from Laura.

Pouring himself a generous Scotch, Bryant lay back and tried to fathom just why *Steambuffs'* secretary found it so easy to resist his charms. Okay, he was a lot older and certainly not blessed with film star looks, but he *had* made something of his life and, in spite of a few run-ins with the law, managed to set up *Heritage Engineering*, now an established source of reproduction parts for old engines.

It hadn't been an easy road to such success and certainly not as smooth as he would have his customers believe. Perhaps he was stretching it a bit to tell them he'd trained with Rolls Royce, but he'd always found it wasn't what you were, but what people *thought* you were, that counted. And it *was* true that he'd cut his commercial teeth in the automotive industry, though by selling bogus car parts from his van at car boot sales rather than any technical know-how. Unfortunately, pure greed and a bitterness towards those with money had led him into deeper criminal pursuits, culminating in three years as a guest of Her Majesty. On release, he'd tried to get back into the car-parts scam, only to find his source from abroad cut by government controls. Never daunted, he'd solved that by getting an ex-con with a workshop to turn out replica components at cut-down prices.

Demand had been such that he'd soon expanded to his own workshop in the Midlands. The only problem had been finding enough skilled workers to man it, but the solution had come from the *New Start* charity. They had newly-released offenders with engineering skills and *Heritage Engineering* was set up, turning out surprisingly good bespoke parts, including some for Lampeter's own steamboat, *Osprey*.

That was how he'd first met Laura, project-managing the restoration of her father's boat and a girl blessed with both looks and brains. Smitten from the start, attempts to make the relationship more personal had met with equally determined rejection. This morning's text had produced the same zero results and Harry realised it was time for a change of tactics.

He'd already been in contact with Dexter Berrington with a view to buying *Pickle*. Getting his own steamboat would certainly help ingratiate him further with the *Steambuffs* lot, but perhaps now he could set his sights even higher. Berrington needed to sell his boat to buy *Osprey*, but as fate had now thrown him an unexpected windfall, why not use it to buy the big boat himself? He knew how much Laura loved that old steamer. Perhaps her affections might come with it.

Bryant got up, poured himself another Scotch and dialled Ralph Lampeter. All in all, this weekend rally could well be a winner all round.

'So, this is the Great Hospital,' said Laura as she and Jack paused before entrance gates leading to a well kept quadrangle surrounded by period buildings. 'It's like a little oasis of history sitting right here in the middle of Norwich.'

'It's certainly unique,' agreed Jack, leading her in and pointing out various notable houses before turning right and continuing along a walkway between medieval buildings signed "Refectory" and "Master's House".'

'"Master"?' queried Laura.

'That's the historic title of the Hospital Chief Executive, and that lovely Gothic stonework ahead forms one of the smallest cloisters in England. They lead to the Hospital church you spotted earlier.'

'Saint Helen's,' recalled Laura, completely spellbound. 'I can't believe I lived in Norwich for three years and didn't even know this existed.'

'Understandable, as it's not open to the public. The only way to visit is by organised tour or knowing someone who lives here.'

'Well, I'm lucky to be able to see it now,' she said, gratefully. 'So, when and why was it first built?'

'Back in 1249 by Bishop Walter de Suffield as a sanctuary for aged priests. Eventually, they also took in the city's poor and needy.' Continuing along the path, they emerged into another large rectangular courtyard where Jack directed Laura towards a long, brick, single storey building bordering the far side. 'That's the Mackintosh Room, converted from the old East Wards.'

'And where the *Telegraph* casualties would have been brought?'

'Almost certainly. It's now a social centre and, in fact, today's the weekly get-together for the residents, which is why this courtyard's so busy.'

It was indeed, not only with elderly residents making their way to the entrance, but also with staff enjoying their break in the spring sunshine, gardeners weeding the flowerbeds and even a couple of maintenance men working on one end of the building.

'I should still be able to get some good shots around them all,' said Laura, pulling an expensive looking camera from her rucksack and starting to click away. 'At least these photos will show the Great Hospital is still a thriving community.'

'Absolutely. The people who live here call it "The Village" and you can see why.'

'I'll take some general scenes as well,' said Laura, panning round the courtyard, 'and send them to the Master. He might want to put them up on a display board ...' suddenly she faltered and let out a gasp. 'Oh my God!' Shakily, she tried to focus on one spot and zoom in with her telephoto lens, '... that can't be... I don't believe it!' She let the camera drop and put a hand to her mouth as though stifling a scream.

'Good grief, Laura. What's the matter?'

But she didn't answer and instead slumped down onto a nearby bench-seat, her gaze fixed ahead. Jack followed her stare, but the scene looked no different to when they'd first arrived. Something though had drained the colour from her face and he put his arm around her trembling shoulders. 'Take it easy and tell me what's spooked you?'

'I'm so sorry.' She seemed to be trying to pull herself together and was clearly feeling embarrassed at creating a scene. 'I don't know what came over me.'

'But something frightened you?'

'Probably just my eyes playing tricks.'

'Well, just relax for a moment or two. Have you got what you want here?'

'I ... I think so.'

'Good, then let's get you a change of scene.'

They retraced their steps back to the main gate where Jack paused to check the colour was coming back to her face. 'Feeling better?'

'Yes, much thanks. Sorry for that.'

'No problem, but you gave *me* a fright back there. Tell me more of what you saw.'

'You'll think I'm stupid.' She shook her head. 'I just over-reacted, that's all. I was probably imagining the whole thing.'

'Imagining what?'

'You won't believe this, but I thought I saw a ghost.'

*   *   *

Walking slowly along Bishopgate towards the Cathedral, Laura didn't elaborate and Jack didn't press the issue. Finally, at the narrow alleyway leading to The Close, she paused to take a deep breath. 'Ah, that feels better.'

'Good, and a cup of tea will help.' Jack nodded ahead. 'I've arranged to meet Audrey here in the refectory for lunch, so come and join us.'

But she shook her head. 'Thanks anyway, Jack, but I feel fine now. I'll walk with you part of the way, but then carry on into the city centre for a bit retail therapy.'

'Good idea.' As they continued, it certainly seemed as though the peace

18

and tranquillity of the setting was working its magic on Laura, who appeared to be brightening with every step. By the time they'd reached the cloisters, she was nearly her old self. 'Sure I can't tempt you?'

'No thanks, Jack. *Osprey* arrives tomorrow and there's lots I need to get for the rally.' That thought alone seemed to have already restored some of her old spark and brought colour back into her cheeks. 'I'm glad you're going to be there. As well as you meeting Dexter, it means I can also introduce you to Jim.'

'Jim Rowston, the boat's engineer you told me about?'

'That's right, and as I mentioned, he was one of Father's released offenders.' She paused to study his reaction. 'Are you okay with that, Jack?'

'Of course. He's paid his dues to society, Laura, and seems to be trying to make something of his life again. That's how I'll judge him.'

She smiled relief. 'Oh, that's great. He'll certainly be proud to show you all he's done on *Osprey*. He's worked wonders with the old boat.'

'Then I'll look forward to seeing it and you, tomorrow.'

They went their separate ways, Laura on through The Close and Jack to his rendezvous with Audrey, but still pondering the morning's strange happening and the ever-more-unusual direction this rally was taking.

*   *   *

'Saw a ghost! Good grief.' In the modern first floor refectory with its vaulted wooden ceiling and sympathetically adjoined original stonework, Audrey had listened wide-eyed to her husband's account of the strange event at the Great Hospital. 'Do you believe her?'

Jack shrugged. 'I believe she saw *something*, Aud, but what, I don't know. Laura never gave the impression of being the hysterical type, but something gave her a nasty shock back there, be it real or imagined.'

'And you didn't press her for more details?'

'I tried, but she didn't want to talk about it.'

'But you saw nothing yourself?'

'Nothing out of the ordinary. There were residents, staff and some contract builders moving around, but they all seemed pretty earthly and twenty-first century to me. Laura obviously spotted *something*, but I can't for the life of me work out what it was.'

'Did she actually photograph it then?'

'I'm not sure. After she'd taken the shots of the East Wards, she seemed to be clicking away until she dropped the camera, so who knows. In all the kerfuffle, I didn't have a chance to look.'

'A pity. She might have got the photo of the year if she really had snapped a ghost … which, of course, she hasn't,' retracted Audrey immediately, 'but Laura's so level-headed. It all sounds so very out-of-character.'

'I agree, but I think there might be a more rational answer, Aud.'

'Which is?'

'That she's become so totally absorbed by the *Telegraph* disaster, as to start imagining flashbacks. Caught up in the old-world atmosphere of the Great Hospital, she may well have simply *thought* she saw the ghostly apparition of one of the victims as she zoomed in to photo the very building they were taken to.'

'Well, goodness knows what she *thought* she saw, but at least she seems to have got over it now, Jack.'

'Yeah, except another problem reared its head even before we got to the Hospital.' Jack related Laura's text from Harry Bryant and his unwanted attentions.

'Oh, dear, even more problems for the poor girl then,' sympathised Audrey. 'This chap doesn't sound the most attractive of suitors.'

'Totally *un*attractive, according to Laura, but I'll find out for myself at the weekend.' Further discussion though was stopped by Jack's attention suddenly being drawn to the large TV screen at the far end of the refectory. A popular feature, it continually showed the scene captured by a webcam 246 feet up the Cathedral spire where, on a specially-constructed nesting platform, a pair of peregrine falcons returned each year to thrill 50,000 cathedral visitors with their latest brood. 'Heh, they've had their chicks!' he exclaimed, marvelling at the sight of a bundle of feathers now moving against the magnificent backdrop of eastern Norwich.

'That's right, two, a couple of weeks ago.' Audrey knew how much her husband enjoyed following their progress. 'Go and have a closer look.'

'Right.' Needing little further prompting, Jack moved closer to the screen, easily identifying as he did so, several outlying landmarks, including the Great Hospital with St Helen's church, the chaplain's house, the old wards and … something else … something moving within the Hospital grounds. Then, in a few seconds, the image had disappeared amongst the sprawling buildings. He stood back, eyes fixed to the screen, hoping to see it again, but it was gone.

He was left pondering if he had really seen what he thought, or was it now *his* imagination that was playing tricks?

*   *   *

Chapter Three

Fog was lying densely over the marshes next morning, as Jack drove into the Stalham Boatyard. Sheds and workshops lay cloaked in eerie precipitation while, beside the long quays, lines of moored cruisers sat still and glistening in the damp windless air. It was only when he turned down the slipping quay that the vast bulk of a steamboat, sitting atop a multi-wheel low-loader, emerged through the murk.

Well aware that all boats look bigger out of the water, Jack was still impressed by *Osprey*'s forty-two foot black steel hull, seemingly filling the quay. Even in this dull light, she looked immaculate, the varnished wooden wheelhouse and main cabin gleaming with condensation and, between them, the black and red funnel rigged down on the cabin top.

Hearing his arrival, Laura appeared from behind the hull, a beaming smile showing through a face streaked with grime and her voice full of the old zeal. 'Morning, Jack. Thanks for coming.'

'My pleasure, and glad to see you've recovered from yesterday's ghostly apparition.'

'Oh, that was just me being silly.' Her eyes were sparkling with a new-found radiance. 'I had a lovely time in the city after I left you, checking out a few of my old haunts and spending more in the shops than I should have done. And now *Osprey*'s here, safe and sound, so come and see her.'

'Ah, that's how a boat should look,' said Jack, admiringly, as they circled the vessel. 'More a little ship, really.' He nodded towards the huge mobile crane standing poised to work its magic. 'I see you've had to hire a heavy-lifter for this job.'

'That's right. *Osprey*'s far too heavy for the boatyard crane to handle. Jim's just checking everything's all set.' As she spoke, a fit-looking man in his mid-thirties broke off conversation with the crane driver, wiped greasy hands on his blue coveralls and came across to join them.

'Good to meet you, Jim,' said Jack, offering his hand.

'And you, Mr Fellows.' The young engineer's handshake was strong, and his voice more assured than Jack would have expected from an ex-con. 'Laura told me you'd be mentoring us through this weekend.'

'I'll be trying to help in any way I can.' Jack glanced towards *Osprey*. 'She looks very smart. I gather that's largely due to you.'

He shrugged, modestly. 'I do my best with the old girl. I'll be glad to show you round when we've got her afloat again.'

'Which should be very soon,' added Laura, hearing the crane's diesel engine throbbing into life. 'These windless conditions are perfect for getting her in.' She gestured towards the headrope already hanging from the bow. 'You take that to steady her, Jack, while Jim handles the sternrope.'

'Right.' Jack jumped into action, at the same realising they were still one short of the expected crew. 'I thought the chap who wanted to buy her ... Dexter Berrington ... was going to be here?'

'Yes, but he sent a text to say he's been delayed.'

'By the fog?'

'More likely by Margo. I think his dear wife resents any time he spends with boats.'

'Well, she's going to have to get used to more of it if he starts a trip-boat business,' chuckled Jack, taking hold of the headrope as the crane started easing *Osprey* off its transporter.

*   *   *

'It's a standard two cylinder compound, Mr Fellows.'

With *Osprey* now safely craned in, lying afloat and warped to the quay, Jim Rowston was showing Jack what was obviously his pride and joy. From the wheelhouse, with its varnished woodwork and shining brass fittings, they'd made their way down through a scuttle hatch into the steamboat's cramped engine-room where Jack was now running admiring eyes over machinery gleaming in a new coat of green paint, the polished blue-metalled cylinders mirroring snow-white lagging and shining copper pipework. 'It's pretty obvious that you have a real love of this boat.'

'I certainly do.' Jim paused to wipe a spot of errant grease from the brass rim of a steam gauge. 'She'd been a bit neglected, so I've spent the last twelve months getting her back in shape.'

'I understand your own life's had a few knocks though,' said Jack, raising a subject he felt best broached from the start. 'But you obviously have some sort of engineering background. Where did that come from?'

'At sea as an apprentice in tankers.' Jim seemed glad to relate a life both good and bad. 'Once I'd got my ticket, I worked up to Second Engineer in a VLCC ...' he paused, his face clouding, '... and then I went and did something stupid.'

'For which you've paid your dues,' reassured Jack. 'And now you're back into marine engineering with a beautifully restored boat to show for it.'

'Thanks to Mr Lampeter and his charity. He gave me a second chance and now I not only have a dream job, but a home too.'

'Yes, I understand you actually *live* on the boat. Bit of a squeeze, isn't it?'

The engineer shrugged. 'Still better than the cell I shared for a year.' He nodded for'ard. 'There's a single bunk-room up in the bow, so I'm cosy enough.'

'That's good then.' Jack tapped the faces of the dormant gauges. 'But I expect you're looking forward to getting her in steam again.'

'Absolutely. That engine might look spic and span ...' he gave it a loving stroke, '... but it's only when super-heated steam starts coming through the main valve that she becomes a living thing.' He glanced topsides. 'First, though, we need some fuel. After that, we'll continue the tow round to the museum and, by tomorrow morning, she'll be all set to steam.'

'And ready for the rally.' Clearly, this was a man whose life now revolved around *Osprey*, which did raise another issue. 'But, after the weekend, Jim, I understand the boat might be sold to Dexter Berrington. How will that leave you?'

'Mr Lampeter said he'd fix me up with a job with Harry Bryant ...' the engineer turned away to re-hang one of his spanners on the bulkhead tool-rack, '... but no way I'm going down that route.'

'But surely a job's a job.'

'Not on his terms, it isn't. I made a mistake once, but I don't intend repeating it.' But, before Jim could explain further, there was a loud bang on the engine-room hatch, followed by Laura's cheerful call.

'Hey, come on you two. The tug's here to take us round to the refuelling point.'

'How about the other boats, Laura?' asked Jack as they climbed back on deck and Jim went to sort lines. 'Are any of them here yet?'

'The three local boats will be making their way to Stalham today or early tomorrow.' She nodded vaguely northwards. 'Mum and Seager are towing *Sunbeam* down the A1 right now. They should be here this afternoon and ready to launch this evening.'

'A long way to come,' said Jack. 'I hope they enjoy driving.'

Laura's smile was only half-humoured. 'Mum never minds, but I'm sure *he's* being a complete pain about the whole thing ... as usual.'

*   *   *

'God, I hate driving on motorways.'

At the wheel of the Land Rover, Charles Seager glanced again in the rear-view mirror to check that *Sunbeam*, their classic twenty-two foot steam launch was still trailing happily behind. It was, but that did nothing to assuage his general discontent. 'Two hundred miles is a heck of a long way for just a weekend rally.'

'It doesn't have to be just the weekend, Charles.' Beside him, Helen Lampeter shifted slightly in her seat. 'Neither of us have been to the Broads before, so after the weekend we could do a bit of exploring on our own.'

'I'll see how I feel then,' grunted Seager, not committing himself.

'Hopefully better than you feel now.' Helen glanced outside to roll her eyes. 'You should just be thankful Ralph isn't coming.'

'Yes, that husband of yours would've been the last straw,' muttered Seager, scowling.

Helen gave her partner a comforting pat on the arm. 'I know how you feel, and I can't stand the man anymore either, but it might have just given us the chance to talk to him again about divorce. After all, you are a lawyer. Surely you could have talked him into some sort of compromise.'

'I'd have been wasting my time,' said Seager, wincing as an articulated lorry came thundering past. He always worried about road damage to *Sunbeam*'s immaculately varnished hull, and mention of Ralph Lampeter didn't help reduce the stress. 'You know as well as I do, Helen, that the man's not going to play ball until you agree to his demands.'

'Which are so damned unreasonable, I won't even consider them.'

'Not even for us?'

'Not when we're happy as we are, but I'd been hoping a face-to-face meeting might at least appeal to his better nature.'

'If he had one ... which he hasn't,' sneered Seager. 'I tell you, Helen, it'll take more than a chat to have us shot of that husband of yours.'

'Yes, well let's just forget him for the moment, shall we, and look forward to a few days afloat in *Sunbeam*,' soothed Helen. 'Laura says the museum we're meeting up at is really interesting and she's booked us into a local hotel for tonight and tomorrow.'

'So, how is Laura?' Seager had a genuine affection for the girl he hoped would soon be his step-daughter, even if it was clouded with secret guilt.

'Fine. When I spoke to her last night she seemed to have got everything sorted for the rally.'

'A lot of hard work though.'

'Yes, but you know how Laura thrives on challenges like that.' Helen gave a little chuckle. 'In fact, she sounded so upbeat on the phone, I couldn't help feeling something had put a spring in her step.'

'Why, what's happened?'

'She didn't say, but I'm looking forward to seeing her again. It seems ages since we had a good catch-up.'

'I'm sure.' Seager shifted in his seat and started to tap the steering wheel.

Helen knew the signs. 'You've been driving for a couple of hours now, Charles, and getting tired. Next service area, pull in and I'll take over.'

'Right.' Seager glanced down at the satnav. 'Halfway there, so good progress.'

'And, hopefully, a smooth run ahead,' said Helen.

Seager silently prayed that would apply to personal matters as well as driving. It all depended on secrets staying just that ... secret. His love for Helen had meant never telling her the full story. He hoped to God she never found out. If she did, her estranged husband wouldn't be the only man she hated.

A service area was coming up and he pulled onto the slip road with another glance at the satnav. Still another hundred miles to Stalham.

*   *   *

Just refuelled and still warped alongside the boatyard tug, *Osprey* was now being slowly repositioned to the museum quay. Standing beside Laura and Jim on the steamboat's foredeck, Jack noticed their bow paying out slightly. 'Probably best if we eased off that sternline and hardened this headrope. The forespring is the one doing most of the work and it's always good to have the bow canted in a bit.'

'Right, I'll look after the stern if you and Jim take care of the bow,' agreed Laura.

With the lines quickly re-hitched, it didn't take long for Jim to see the effect. 'You're right, she's towing lot easier now, Mr Fellows.'

'Good ... and forget the "Mr Fellows" ... the name's Jack.'

'Right ... Jack.' The engineer paused to check the fenders were still doing their job. Seeing they were, he gave a satisfied sigh. 'Give me engines and machinery, and I'm in my element, but I'm still learning to be a seaman.'

'You're doing great, Jim.' They could all relax for the next ten minutes now as steamboat and tug chugged through the boatyard. 'Have you ever been to the Broads before?'

'Never, but I've always wanted to come here and explore the area. From the little I've seen already, it looks a boater's paradise.'

The fog was dissipating now, but enough remained to give the scene an almost ethereal charm. 'A pity you can't carry on maintaining *Osprey* here in Norfolk.'

'Yes, I'd love to, but I'm sure Dexter will be doing it all himself to save money.'

'Did you know each other in the Merchant Navy?'

'Only *of* him. A good ship-handler, I heard, and destined for promotion. Goodness knows why he gave it all up to run an art gallery with a pushy wife.'

'Have you met Margo then?'

'No, but some of his old shipmates did and weren't too impressed.' The engineer shrugged. 'Ah well, we all make mistakes, but at least he's doing something to rectify his.'

They were approaching the museum moorings now, the tug slowing and hands getting ready to let go the tow once alongside. Jim glanced aft to check Laura was ready to slip her line, before taking off a few turns of the headrope.

'Right, I'll look after the spring,' offered Jack, making his way to the stern. They were edging alongside the museum quay now where a tall, clean-cut figure in tan trousers and blue waterproof stood watching. He'd doubtless soon be forming his own opinion of Dexter Berrington.

* * *

'You've done a good job, Jim.' In *Osprey*'s small wheelhouse, her prospective new owner scanned the immaculate interior and gave an approving nod. 'She looks great.'

Within minutes of coming aboard, Dexter's keen eyes had been checking the boat's every detail, nodding approval here or voicing thoughts on how things might be improved yet further there. Some might have taken umbrage at this, but the ex-mariner's obvious expertise in all things nautical, at least created a grudging acceptance in Jim Rowston.

'Glad you like her.' He nodded towards the engine-room scuttle. 'If you're finished with me, I've got jobs to do in readiness for steaming tomorrow.'

Dexter nodded. 'Of course. Carry on.'

'A good man,' said Jack, as the engineer disappeared below.

'Yes, I can see that from the brilliant job he's done on this boat.'

'Certainly not the type you'd expect to have done time in prison,' said Jack, confidentially. 'Do you know what that was for?'

'We never served on the same ship,' said Dexter, 'but the story I heard was that they caught him with a stash of drugs on return from the Far East. Not being a user himself, they suspected he was dealing and gave him a correspondingly longer sentence.'

'What was his defence?'

'He didn't have one, and simply pleaded guilty.'

'Hmm, well he's paid the price and seems intent now on making amends.' Jack gave *Osprey*'s varnished wheel a thump. 'He's certainly feeling the wrench of parting from this boat.'

'I can understand that. He's put his heart and soul into looking after her.'

'No way you can take him on?'

'Afraid not. I'd like to, but just buying this old girl is going to take every penny I've got ... that's if I even end up owning her at all.'

Before he could explain further, Laura appeared in the wheelhouse doorway. 'I've just brewed some coffee in the saloon if you two are ready.'

'Sounds good. Are you joining us?'

'No, I'm off into the museum to chat with the curator about mooring arrangements for the other boats.'

Making their way aft, ranger and ex-mariner were soon descending the two steps down into *Osprey*'s wood-panelled saloon where brass lamps and velvet-covered couches completed a vision of opulent yesteryear. At the for'ard end, the open-plan galley was divided from the rest of the saloon by a polished mahogany counter, above which cut-glass tumblers and wine glasses were secured in crafted holders. On the counter itself, Laura had placed white cups and saucers, sugar, milk and a pot of freshly brewed coffee.

'Wow, they certainly do things in style in *Osprey* don't they?' said Jack, pouring two coffees while at the same time admiring the pot itself with the initial *O* engraved onto its silver-plated side. 'Georgian, if I'm not mistaken, but a bit posh for using when she's a trip boat.'

'Don't worry, Jack, the contents aren't included,' explained Dexter, taking his coffee to a small table between two armchairs. 'Like I said, it's not certain if I'll even end up buying the boat. There are a few details still to be finally hammered out ... like price.'

'Really? I had the impression the deal was almost done.'

'That's what I'd hoped, but when I spoke to Ralph Lampeter last night he said someone else was making an offer.'

'That's bad luck. A pity he's not going to be here this weekend so you could thrash it out with him.'

'Quite.' Dexter took a sip of coffee while looking at Jack curiously over the rim. 'So, you've heard I'm planning to start a trip-boat operation in Norwich?'

'Yes, Laura told me. You're obviously dead keen to get back into the marine business.'

'Too true, I am. I'd still be at sea now if I hadn't gone and married Margo.'

'She was already a friend of Laura's wasn't she?'

'Yes, they met in the Sainsbury Art Centre on the university campus when Laura was at UEA and Margo at Norwich School of Art. They were the best of friends for a while.'

'But not any longer?'

'Oh, you know how it is, Jack ... people move on in life. Laura developed other interests, Margo got her own gallery, and they just drifted apart.'

'Well, I should think running a successful business is pretty time-consuming,' placated Jack, 'so I can see how the friendship slipped.'

'I don't know about the "successful" bit,' said Dexter, dejectedly. '*ArtVu* sometimes goes days without a single customer ... and probably a good thing, as Margo hasn't painted anything for years. Her artwork sold well, but the ones we have in the shop now are amateurish and no-one wants to buy them.'

'And yet, *ArtVu* keeps its head above water.'

'Only from the money Margo's other business brings in.'

'Which is?'

'To be honest, I've never been quite sure. Something to do with antiques, but she keeps that side well under her hat. So, I'm landed with running the shop all day while she's out and about wheeling and dealing. We don't talk about it – in fact we seldom talk, full-stop – but she just says one of us needs to earn a living.'

'Well, she's obviously done well to find a profitable sideline,' said Jack, still trying to throw some positive aspects into this strange relationship. 'I'm sorry I won't be meeting her at the rally.'

'Ah, but you will be, because she's changed her mind and has now decided to come.'

'Really?' Jack tried not to look too surprised. 'I got the impression she wasn't interested in boats.'

'Certainly hasn't been before,' admitted Dexter, 'but now she's almost desperate to be here this weekend.'

'What's caused the change in heart?'

'I wish I knew, but it has to be linked to something odd that happened in *ArtVu* a couple of days ago.' Dexter went on to explain the strange incident that had left his wife distracted and nervy and concluded by saying, 'I understand you were once a policeman, Jack, so perhaps you might make some sense of it.'

'It's certainly a puzzler. You say all she'd seen was a man looking through the gallery window. Isn't that something that happens all the time?'

'Of course, but in this instance, Margo looked as if she'd seen a ghost.'

Jack looked up from his coffee. 'A ghost?'

'Yeah, I know it sounds ridiculous, but that's how she reacted.'

'But she didn't explain why she'd found the man so frightening?'

'Couldn't or wouldn't. Whichever, in the end she calmed down and tried to convince me she'd just been silly.'

Jack was thinking of the last time he'd heard a young woman utter those same words. 'But you think it's still worrying her?'

Dexter took a sip of his coffee and nodded sadly. 'I'm sure of it. That's why I was late this morning. She insisted I stay with her until our girl help arrived.'

'Is she normally nervous like this?'

'Absolutely not. Until now, Margo was the most self-assured woman I'd ever met.' He pulled a face. 'Perhaps a bit too self-assured at times.'

Jack sensed it was time to lighten the mood. 'Well, it'll be good to have her with you tomorrow. Perhaps, when she sees *Osprey* for herself, she'll be more enthusiastic about your venture. How will *she* feel about selling *Pickle*?'

'I think she'll just be glad to see the back of her.' Dexter seemed close to adding, "and me", but didn't.

'Well, *I'm* looking forward to seeing *Pickle* myself.'

Dexter visibly brightened. 'She's a lovely boat, but only nineteen foot six, and basically just an open launch with a steam engine, so way too small for the passenger operation I have in mind.' He paused to savour *Osprey*'s varnished opulence. 'That's why I'm so keen to purchase this one.'

'And I think you'll be onto a winner,' encouraged Jack. 'Okay, boiler inspections are going to make your MCA surveys more involved but, as long as everything's well-maintained, it should be worth it because people love connections to yesteryear and particularly anything steam-powered. Perhaps we can have a talk about it all later, Dexter, because I'd like to see it work out for you.'

'Thanks, Jack. Good to know there's someone who doesn't think I'm completely mad.'

At least not in your choice of boats, thought Jack as Laura entered the saloon with a far-from-happy expression. 'Dexter, I've just had another text from that infernal man, Bryant. It seems that not only is he intending to buy your *Pickle*, but now he's also bidding for *Osprey*.'

'So, *he's* the other one who's made an offer.'

'Looks like it, and of all the people I'd hate this boat to go to, it's him.'

Laura seemed to be almost taking the news worse than Dexter. 'As a member, he's a big enough pain, but as an owner he'd be impossible.'

'... and of, possibly, *two* boats,' completed Jack, suspiciously. 'For an ex-con running a small engineering business, he seems pretty flush with cash.'

'Which is more than I am,' said Dexter, 'and if I go upping my bid he'll probably back out of buying *Pickle*, which would count me out anyway.'

'You mustn't give up though,' declared Laura. 'One way or another, we need *you* to be the one who gets this boat. I'll make sure he sits next to you at the dinner on Saturday evening. That way you might hammer something out between you and I won't have to put up with his lecherous comments.'

'Bryant on one side and Margo on the other,' said Dexter with little enthusiasm. 'That sounds a bundle of fun.'

'Margo?'

'Yes. I haven't had a chance to tell you yet that Margo will be with us after all.'

'She'll be *what?*' There was a hardness in Laura's voice now, mixed with an edge of desperation. 'You surely can't bring *her*, Dexter. Margo hates boats and everything to do with them.'

'Of course I can bring her ... she's my wife. Try and understand, Laura. Just accept the past's the past and that people change.'

'That woman will *never* change, Dexter, so just keep her well clear of me.'

With Laura gone in a cloud of discontent, Dexter turned to Jack and pulled a face. 'Oh dear, seems I've set the cat amongst the pigeons.'

'More like two cats fighting,' corrected Jack. 'Care to explain?'

'Some other time.' Dexter jumped up and emptied the remains of his coffee down the galley sink. 'It's a long story, Jack, and I've enough on my mind right now without digging up all that old dirt.'

*   *   *

'Tea up, Jack.'

'Thanks, love.' Jack switched off his laptop and joined Audrey in the conservatory where his favourite brew and freshly made scones lay waiting on the low table. Lying between the two chairs, Spike stretched contently as Jack gave the collie a rub with his foot before taking a welcome sip. 'Ah, I need this. Being on that laptop has given me a headache.'

'I'm not surprised, the time you've spent on it. What were you looking up?'

'*New Start.*'

'Laura's father's charity?'

'That's right. On the face of it, it seems a reasonable cause. On release, offenders are put in contact with the charity who then try to match them to suitable employers.'

'It certainly sounds worthwhile,' said Audrey, though detecting degrees of enthusiasm in her husband. 'Surely anything that cuts down re-offending must be a good thing.'

Jack helped himself to a scone. 'Absolutely, Aud, except I do question the wisdom of some of the places they send them to. Harry Bryant's *Heritage Engineering* for instance.'

'The firm that makes engine parts for *Steambuffs*? What's wrong with that?'

'Nothing really, I suppose, except Bryant himself is an ex-con.'

'... who probably appreciates more than anyone, the problems facing ex-prisoners back in society.'

'Yeah, you're probably right, love,' conceded Jack. 'Whatever, the programme obviously costs a bit to run, as *New Start's* website explains they even accommodate their clients when first released. No wonder they have an on-going appeal for donations.'

'It can't be easy with so many other worthwhile causes needing funds, Jack. Perhaps that's the reason Ralph Lampeter's selling *Osprey*.'

'Which itself has generated a bit of discontent in the *Steambuffs'* camp,' said Jack, before going on to explain the revelations of the morning.

'Oh dear, not good news for poor Dexter then. What's *he* like?'

'The sort of go-ahead type you'd expect of someone who's held a master's ticket. He obviously misses that old life, and this boat trip business would be right up his street.' Jack put down his cup and frowned. 'He didn't admit it of course, but I suspect it's also a way of escaping an unhappy marriage. I haven't met his wife Margo yet, but she sounds a bit like Winston Churchill described the Russians.'

'"A riddle, wrapped in a mystery, inside an enigma"?'

'Exactly. Dexter told me she's always been very self-assured – too much so, in fact – and yet, what seemed like a quite normal situation, made her completely freak out.' Jack related the strange happening at *ArtVu*.

'Good grief, that almost sounds like a replay of Laura's experience.'

'Doesn't it just ... except Margo's happened the day before.'

'How bizarre.' Audrey put down her cup. 'So, who ... or what ... is it that's giving these girls such a shock?'

'Who knows, seeing as neither of them seem that keen to give details? Dexter reckons it could just have been a weirdo staring in at her.'

'You didn't tell him about Laura's own fright.'

'No.'

'But you think the two incidents might be connected?'

'Difficult to see how.' Jack paused to pour himself another cuppa. 'How would anyone know Laura was going to be at the Great Hospital that morning when *we'd* only arranged it the day before?'

'...or that Margo would be in her gallery, if *she'd* only just returned like Dexter said,' pointed out Audrey. 'The only thing in common with both incidents, as far as I can see, are the girls themselves.'

'... who obviously want nothing to do with each other, Aud. In fact, when Laura found out that Margo was coming to the rally after all, she went ballistic. It's pretty obvious she can't stand the woman now.'

Audrey frowned. 'There's clearly been more than a trivial falling-out between those two, and Dexter's obviously very unhappy ... and who can wonder, with a wife who sounds an absolute nightmare to live with. I think it's him we need to feel sorry for.'

'Yeah, it's obvious he bitterly regrets giving up life at sea. He's just not the type to be stuck in a city selling paintings. Which raises the question of how Margo ever set the gallery up in the first place. Where would a youngster, fresh out of art college, find the money to do that?'

'Selling her paintings, perhaps?'

'Doubtful. Dexter said she was good, but she would never have had the volume of sales to take on that sort of commitment. And he reckons she hasn't painted anything in years and that *ArtVu* only keeps going with the cash her other business brings in.'

'Doing what?'

'Some form of antique trading, apparently, but even Dexter's not sure. I tried checking myself just now on the internet, but drew a blank except for *ArtVu*'s website.'

Audrey shook her head. 'This *Steambuffs* lot certainly seem shrouded in all sorts of mysteries, Jack. But I certainly think Dexter needs to put his foot down and insist on knowing what his wife's up to.'

'I honestly don't think he cares enough to bother, Aud, especially as he won't be lumbered with running the gallery for much longer if his plan works out.'

' "*If* ",' stressed Audrey, 'and we don't know enough about any of them to form firm opinions ...' she gave an increasingly desperate Spike a quick pat, '... but I do know this poor dog is overdue his walk, so let's forget other people's business and get ourselves some fresh air.'

Ten minutes, and all three were following the path by the river, Spike happily running ahead and Jack absent-mindedly watching a hire cruiser making its slow way against the tidal flow. Audrey could guess the way his mind was working. 'You're still thinking of that lovely old boat you were on this morning aren't you?'

'*Osprey?*' Jack came back to the present. 'Yeah, Jim's done a lovely job of restoring her. A shame that, when she's sold, he's going to lose both his work and home.'

'But surely Ralph Lampeter's *New Start* can fix him up with something else?'

'Only a job with this Harry Bryant chappie, which he's dead set against.'

'Perhaps it's not something he'd choose, Jack,' said Audrey, pausing to throw Spike a stick, 'but he should still be grateful for all that *New Start*'s done for him.'

'And he said he is is, Aud, and yet somehow his gratitude rang hollow.'

'How do you mean?'

'Oh, I'm not sure myself yet, but ...'

'... you're suspicious about something,' completed Audrey. 'Oh dear, Jack, this doesn't bode well for a happy atmosphere this weekend. Obviously poor Laura's really riled that not only is this odious Harry Bryant making a bid for her beloved *Osprey*, but that Margo's decided to join them as well. Thank goodness her mum's going to be there to support her, along with her partner ...?'

'... Seager ... Charles Seager. And that's another strange thing, Aud.'

'In what way?'

'Just that when we first chatted with Laura over coffee at the museum, she said how much she liked him.'

'That's right. She didn't go into detail, but gave the impression they got on well.'

'Quite. Well talking to her yesterday, she seemed to have changed her tune and was quite scathing about him.'

'But didn't say why?'

'No, and, as far as I know, she hasn't spoken to him between those two conversations ... unless...'

Audrey immediately recognised that look on her husband's face. 'Another light-bulb moment, Jack?'

'What? Oh, more like a candle-flicker, Aud, but a possible solution that opens a whole new can of worms.'

He didn't elaborate and Audrey didn't push it, for the moment content to just enjoy this blissful stroll by the river well away from others' troubles.

This weekend, though, might be another matter. Something was niggling at Jack and she just prayed events didn't turn nasty.

*   *   *

Chapter Four

Trouble was something seemingly far away the next morning as Jack brought his patrol launch into the museum moorings. It was the first day of the rally and, thankfully, one of fair weather, the anti-cyclonic gloom of the previous days having given way to a bright fresh breeze that ruffled the bunting flying from the museum buildings.

Also carried on that breeze was the nostalgic smell of *Falcon*'s coal smoke. Nearby, the funnels of *Osprey* and the other steamboats also shimmered above newly-lit boilers as they too got up steam for the day ahead. Being oil fired, none of these boats were producing as much smoke as *Falcon*, but still adding their own evocative sense of yesteryear to a scene already being enjoyed by the steam enthusiasts now thronging the museum quay.

Jack avoided the main quay, and instead moored close by a smart black-hulled regatta launch he recognised, along with the boiler-suited figure tending her midships engine and boiler.

'Morning, Dexter.'

'Hi Jack. I've just finished repacking the stuffing box and my hands are filthy, but do come on board.'

Supported by brass stanchions, *Pickle*'s light blue awning was punctured only by her black enamel funnel, producing just enough smoke to drift over the red ensign flying aft. Settling himself into one of the cockpit cushions just ahead of the side-mounted brass wheel, Jack glanced around in admiration. 'Lovely boat, Dexter.'

'Thanks.' He wiped his hands on an old towel. 'Glad you like her.'

'No First Mate yet though?'

'Margo? She's just having a look around the museum.'

'I didn't think she was that interested in old boats.'

'Never was before,' admitted Dexter, 'but I have a feeling she's got some secret agenda here this weekend. I don't know what, but something's still distressing her. All I know is that it involves money, because she's asked if I can help her out.'

'I thought she had her own income?'

'She does, but it seems she suddenly needs more.'

35

'But she hasn't said why?'

'No, and it didn't help when I told her all my savings were set aside for buying *Osprey*.'

'I can imagine how that went down,' sympathised Jack, 'but try and put it to one side and enjoy the rally.' He scanned again the boat's pristine condition, her gleaming varnish work, cheesed-down ropes and neatly stowed gear. '*Pickle*'s certainly not appropriately named.'

Dexter forced a smile. 'This is the way I'll have *Osprey* ... if she's ever mine.'

'Any progress there?'

'No, nothing more heard from Ralph Lampeter, so I thought I might talk to the boat's original owner.'

'Who's that?'

'Helen Lampeter.' Dexter was indicating the slightly larger all-varnished regatta launch lying further down the quay. As immaculate as *Pickle*, the boat had the added benefit of an aft cabin and a solid canopy over the for'ard cockpit, boiler and engine. Gold scrolled on its graceful bow was the name: *Sunbeam*. 'She and Charles got here yesterday afternoon and craned straight in.'

'But you said "the boat's original owner"?'

'That's right.' Dexter glanced about to check no-one was within hearing. 'You see *Osprey*, together with a substantial amount of money, was inherited by Helen from *her* side of the family.'

'So, how come she doesn't have the boat now?'

'Good question, but we all suspect she gave it to Ralph as a form of peace offering when they split. The way we understand it, RLC had just gone bust and Ralph probably smelled a large settlement in his favour if they divorced. Helen was equally determined he wouldn't, so there's something of a stand-off...'

'... with *Osprey* in the middle,' surmised Jack.

'Exactly, but Ralph's got the upper hand, knowing that Helen's keen for a divorce to marry Seager.'

'But until then, they're still technically married, meaning Helen still has some entitlement to ownership of the boat.'

'That's what I'm banking on,' said Dexter with a wink. 'I have a hunch she'd like me to have *Osprey*.'

'Does she know about Bryant's offer?'

'I'm not sure, but I can't think she'd be very happy at the prospect.'

'But Bryant's still interested in buying *Pickle*, I hope?'

'That's what he told me fifteen minutes ago before he went off to chat up

Laura.'

'Bad luck her, but why on earth does he want *two* steamboats?'

Dexter shrugged. 'Goodness knows. *Osprey's* way too big to run as a private boat.'

'Nevertheless, a boat much loved by Laura,' said Jack, thinking aloud. 'You don't think he sees owning her as a way to the girl's heart.'

'Could do. That man's slippery enough to try anything, especially if it concerns Laura.'

'I think any ambition he's got there is doomed to failure though,' said Jack with a smile, 'and let's hope his bid for *Osprey* suffers the same fate. But good luck with Helen.' He glanced towards *Sunbeam*, and the figures appearing in her cockpit. 'Time for me to go and meet her in person.'

'Good idea. I think Laura and Charles are with her, but for God's sake don't mention a word of what I've just told you.'

Having promised, Jack took his leave and wandered off down the quay to where *Sunbeam* lay gleaming in the morning sunshine. One thing you couldn't fault *Steambuffs* for, he mused, was the care they lavished on their beautiful boats. In fact, they seemed to love them more than each other. It remained to be seen whether that was good or bad.

*   *   *

'Jack ... good to see you.'

Laura was relaxing in *Sunbeam's* cockpit, nursing a mug of coffee and chatting to the attractive lady in her late fifties sitting beside her. 'Come on board and meet Mum.'

'Would love to ... thanks.'

Jack climbed aboard, stepping carefully over the varnished gunwale and into the cockpit where the boat's machinery seemed more an embellishment than an intrusion. Nearby, the boiler was encased in brass-rimmed mahogany, its emissions venting up through the white enamelled funnel and its steam all set to feed the small two-cylinder compound engine just ahead of the cabin.

Helen Lampeter stood up, hand outstretched. 'Hello, Jack, I've just been hearing all about you.' Her short dark hair was peppered with grey, but still thick and stylish while the blue eyes beneath flashed with youthful zest. 'And this is my partner, Charles.'

A slightly-built man of about the same age had just emerged from the aft cabin.

'Pleased to meet you, Jack.'

'And you, Charles. I understand you're a lawyer.'

But it was Laura who responded. '*Was* a lawyer, Jack. These days he finds it easier to live off his wife.' She gave a little laugh as though joking, but the barb behind it was clear enough for Helen to spin around.

'Laura, that's unkind.' She turned quickly back to Jack. 'Sorry about this. We're not normally at each other's throats.'

'That's okay,' assured Jack, conscious that the atmosphere on this boat was building quicker than the steam pressure. 'And, anyway, looks like you've got some interested public.'

Thankfully, a small group of visitors had just paused to admire the boat and clearly keen to ask some questions. Helen gave them a cheerful smile. 'Ah, good morning, steam enthusiasts. Welcome to *Sunbeam*. What can I tell you?'

'Load of nosey-parkers if you ask me,' muttered Seager to Jack. 'Not something I want to take part in, so I'm off to look around the museum.'

'Thank God for that,' murmured Laura with feeling as her prospective step-father scuttled off in the direction of the main display buildings. She gave one of her old smiles and nodded towards Helen, now fully engaged with her audience. 'Mum'll be chatting away for ages, so let me show you the other boats and introduce you to their owners.'

'Righteo.' With the town brass band now adding to the festive mood and a local TV crew preparing to record the event, they made their way along the quay, which was getting more crowded by the minute. Alongside *Osprey*, Jim Rowston was explaining the workings of his pride and joy. 'There's a man happy in his work.'

Laura nodded. 'Yes, and thankfully far better with people than my mother's choice of man.'

'There seems a bit of tension between you and Charles now,' probed Jack. 'You initially gave the impression you liked him.'

'Did I?' Laura frowned. 'Ah well, if Mum wants to make the same mistake twice, that's up to her. Anyway, let's move on and meet the other rally members.'

By now they were beside *Whisper*, an open white-painted clinker-built launch that Laura explained was owned by Lionel Hillbeck, the local farmer whose steam traction engine would be giving demonstrations at How Hill the following day. The man himself seemed a jovial enough character, appropriately dressed in period costume and giving a welcoming wave from onboard as he happily buffed up the copper pipework of his engine. Similarly attired, his wife, suitably shaded by a colourful parasol, called across, 'Hi, Laura. See you later at Sutton Staithe.'

'Will do, Pat. Just make sure your Victorian roll-play doesn't extend to alcoholic abstinence.'

'Don't worry, it won't.'

'Pat's good fun,' said Laura as they moved on. 'I'll make sure she's next to you at tonight's dinner.'

'Thanks.' Jack glanced back at *Whisper*'s completely open length. 'Presumably, the Hillbecks won't be sleeping onboard.'

'No, their sons will be running them too-and-fro each day. Doctor Edwards and Eileen will be sleeping on theirs though.' Laura was pointing to the last steamboat on display, a magnificent twenty-six foot launch with a small cabin amidships. '*Patience* was originally an umpire's launch on the Thames that Doc has spent his retirement renovating.' A slightly Pickwickian-type figure in the cockpit smiled and gave a mock salute.

'If he cared for his patients as much as he does his boat, they must have been sorry to see him go,' said Jack, returning the salute before turning back along the quay. Passing *Osprey*, he noticed the boat's engineer was still happily chatting to visitors. 'How about Jim ... will he be at the meal with us tonight?'

Laura shook her head. 'No. I did invite him, but he said he fancied a run ashore, so he's off to Yarmouth for the evening. I don't blame him ... by then he'll probably have had enough of steam engine talk for one day.'

'Probably,' agreed Jack. 'What are you doing now?'

'Oh, going for a look around the museum while I have the chance and then popping to see the curator to thank her for having us. How about you?'

'I'll go and see how Dexter's getting on.'

Wandering back down the quay, Jack considered Jim Rowston's decision to spend the evening in Yarmouth. In some ways it was strange that he'd pass up the chance of a good meal, though a few hours amongst the holidaymakers on the prom would probably be more fun.

Fun, though, was not something Charles Seager seemed to be enjoying when Jack came back abeam *Sunbeam*. For the lawyer was sitting slumped on a bench seat close-by looking decidedly white and shaken. As Jack stopped to help, Helen appeared from their boat with a large tumbler of brandy. 'I don't know what happened,' she blurted out, holding the tumbler to her partner's lips. 'He was like this when he came back from the museum. Something there seemed to really upset him.'

Jack put a hand on the man's trembling shoulder. 'Charles, what on earth's the matter?'

'What ...?' he stammered, trying to pull himself together, '... oh, just had a bit of a shock, that's all.'

Helen frowned. 'Obviously more than "a bit". You look like you've just seen a ghost.'

Charles looked up pathetically and shook his head. 'Perhaps I have, Helen ... perhaps I have.'

*   *   *

'What's the matter with old Seager?' Back on board *Pickle*, Dexter had obviously watched the mini-drama.

'Bit of a mystery,' answered Jack. 'He hinted at seeing a ghost in the museum but, other than that, didn't want to talk about it.'

Dexter frowned. 'Strange. I'd have thought he was a pretty down-to-earth sort of chap. What do *you* think it was?'

'I have no idea, but something certainly put the wind up him. I expect all will be revealed in time.'

'Probably, but talking of unwelcome apparitions, look who's here.'

Jack followed Dexter's scowl to the rather short, stocky man strolling up the quay and soon placing a hard-soled shoe on *Pickle*'s varnished gunwale.

'Afternoon, Dexter. I see you're busy sprucing up the old girl.'

'Hello, Harry.' It was time for introductions. 'Jack, this is Harry Bryant who's buying *Pickle*.'

'*Possibly* buying,' corrected Bryant. 'We'll see how I feel after I've tried her out.'

'Right, well you'd better come aboard then.'

Pickle's cockpit seemed all the smaller and certainly less cheery with Bryant on board. From one of the cockpit side seats, he turned an enquiring eye on Jack. 'What did you say your name was?'

'I didn't, but it's Jack Fellows ... Broads Ranger.' Already feeling that a little bit of Harry Bryant would go a long way, Jack didn't offer his hand.

'Not here to spoil our fun, I hope.' Harry gave a silly little laugh.

'Not if you all keep to the rules of the river. I understand you make parts for steamboats?'

'That and other precision engineering.' He swept an arrogant hand over *Pickle*'s gleaming engine. 'I've certainly kept that bag of old nails running over the years, haven't I Dexter?'

'You've made a *few* parts for the boat, Harry ... yes.'

'And, I gather, for *Osprey* as well,' pressed Jack, nodding towards the big old steamer close by.

'Absolutely.' Bryant leaned a little closer in mock confidence. 'It's me they can thank for her looking as good as she does.'

'Oh, really?' Jack's eyes narrowed slightly. 'I thought Jim Rowston had done most of the restoration?'

'What, the paid hand?' Bryant gave an audible snort. 'He wouldn't be there now if Ralph Lampeter hadn't felt sorry for him. A pity the boss won't be here this weekend though, because there's something I need to chat to him about?'

'Is that so?' said Dexter through gritted teeth. 'Well, you're out of luck there, I'm afraid.'

'No problem. Perhaps I'll just chat with his gorgeous daughter instead.'

'Not a good idea either, Harry. She's got enough on right now running this rally without having to find time for you.'

'Not that she ever has much time for anyone, especially old friends.' The words came from a shapely young woman who'd just appeared on the quay. Wearing tight jeans and totally inappropriate high-heels, Jack had little doubt as to who she was.

'Jack ... meet Margo,' introduced Dexter with little apparent enthusiasm as his wife clambered awkwardly aboard with even less.

Plonking herself down on one of the side-bench cushions, Margo glanced around the launch with a contemptuous sniff of the funnel exhaust. 'God, what pleasure do people get being on these smelly old things? Are we ready to go?'

'Not quite. Steamboats aren't like cars, Margo ... they do need some preparation.'

'So, not a steam enthusiast yourself?' asked Jack, tongue in cheek.

Margo didn't answer immediately, but managed to turn and raise her sunglasses in Jack's direction. 'What business is it of yours?'

'Jack's looking after our little flotilla this weekend,' explained Dexter, casting an apologetic look towards the ranger.

'Really?' Without further attempt at conversation, she popped back her sunglasses before pulling a glossy fashion magazine from her bag and burying her face in its pages.

'Right, I'll go see Laura for any last minute details of our move to Sutton,' said Jack, hopping thankfully ashore.

Heading for the museum buildings, he couldn't help pondering on the volatile mix of personalities this rally had brought together. That and the fact that Margo Berrington hadn't even attempted to make eye-contact with Harry Bryant.

*   *   *

41

'The moorings are all booked at Sutton Staithe,' said Laura when Jack joined her and her mum, who were standing outside one of the museum's display sheds, 'but perhaps it would be a good idea if you went on ahead and checked all's okay. We'll follow as a flotilla when we've wrapped up here.'

'No problem. Perhaps by then there'll be a bit more amity in *Pickle*'s crew.'

'Yes, poor Dexter, stuck with both that dreadful wife of his *and* Bryant.' She ran a hand nervously through her hair and glanced about distractedly. 'Anyway, I've got enough to think about without concerning myself with those two.'

'Is something worrying you, Laura?'

'What? ... oh, no ...' she forced a smile, '... just Charles ... thinking he'd seen something.'

Looking for a more balanced explanation, Jack turned to Helen. 'How is our ghost-spotter?'

'He'll be fine.' She seemed far less concerned than her daughter. 'Just his nerves playing up again. I gave him another good swig of best Napoleon, which seems to have done the trick.'

'Yes, but in no state to be crewing for you around to Sutton,' said Laura, forcing her mind back to practicalities. 'I know it's not far, but shall I ask Bryant to go along with you as deckhand?'

'Good Lord no!' protested an emphatic Helen. 'I'd rather sail solo around the world than have five minutes with that man. I've handled *Sunbeam* alone before, so that short leg will be nothing.'

'If you're sure,' relented Laura, 'I'll tell Bryant, to stay in *Pickle* and that way Dexter can do a sales job en route.'

'Okay, but perish the thought that dreadful man ever becomes an owner.' Helen shook her head. 'If he does, *Steambuffs* could be stuck with him for good.'

'Not a happy prospect for me or the group,' agreed Laura, 'but did you know he's also expressed an interest in buying *Osprey*?'

'What!' Helen took a step back. 'I can't believe even Ralph would be so heartless as to sell that lovely boat to the likes of him. No wonder your father's giving this rally a miss ... he knows what a mouthful he'd get from me.' She put her hands on her hips. 'Well, we'll see about that.'

Laura nodded. 'Just forget him for now, Mum, and look forward to our dinner tonight and a pleasant stay in the hotel.'

'You're not sleeping on board then?' queried Jack.

Helen shook her head. 'No, worst luck. I'd have been glad to, but Charles isn't keen.'

'Probably best,' said Laura, dismissively. 'A bit of relaxation might at least take his mind off imaginary sightings.'

A sentiment Laura could well adopt herself, thought Jack as he took his leave and headed for the museum offices.

*   *   *

'I'm off soon and the rest will follow in about an hour, Nicola.' Jack was with the museum curator. 'I think Laura came earlier to thank you herself.'

But the curator shook her head. 'No, I haven't seen her since early this morning ... but that doesn't matter ... I'm sure she's been up to her neck sorting out everything else.'

'Well, it's been a brilliant day and we really appreciate all the effort you've put into making it such a success.'

'No problem, Jack. It's good publicity for the museum and it was fun to have you all here.'

Jack turned to go, but then paused. 'Oh, just one other thing. It may seem an odd question, Nicola, but does the museum have a ghost?'

*   *   *

Chapter Five

'You're kidding, Jack. Not *another* ghost?'

Having arrived at Sutton Staithe in good time for the evening "do", Audrey had sat open-mouthed listening to Jack's account of the strange incident at the museum. They were at one of the hotel's outside tables enjoying a drink as the rest of the flotilla arrived, but she was somewhat bemused at hearing of yet another strange encounter.

'That's what Charles reckoned,' said Jack after a welcome glug of his lager. 'Of course, it had to be something more earthly.' He glanced down the staithe to where the steamboats were all now lying at their moorings, wisps of smoke and steam coiling upwards from their funnels as boilers cooled in the still of the evening. 'Whatever it was certainly shook him up, though he didn't seem keen to elaborate ... at least not to me.'

'But that's three very strange incidents in three different locations in just a matter of days, Jack. What on earth's going on?'

'Goodness knows. Perhaps it really *isn't* "earthly" at all.'

'Now, don't tell me even *you* think they might be ghosts,' scorned Audrey.

'Of course I don't, but every staithe and hamlet in Broadland seems to have its own unique spooky tale. I had a word with the curator at the museum and, sure enough, there is a ghost myth associated with the place. Apparently, two knights from their tombs up the road are supposed to come to the staithe every year and do battle with a Saracen.'

'The clue there, Jack, is in the word "myth",' said Audrey, looking over the rim of her glass. 'Definitely not the sort of apparitions who'd pay a visit to a steamboat rally in broad daylight, bother to wander into Norwich to frighten Laura or stare through Margo Berrington's gallery window.'

'I'm well aware of that, love, which makes it all the more difficult to see how they could possibly be related.' Jack swirled the remains of his lager around in his glass. 'I'm determined to get to the bottom of it all before the rally's over, though.'

'And I'm sure you won't rest until you do, Jack,' said Audrey with mounting despair, 'but can we try and forget it for at least this evening. Judging by the coverage I watched on the local news before leaving home, the day at the museum's been a great success, so everyone should be in good spirits.'

'Ah, yes, I saw the TV crew there. I'd have liked to see the report myself.'

'Well, you still can, Jack, because I recorded it just in case.'

'Ah, that's good, love ... and, yes, the day went really well with loads of visitors and a good friendly atmosphere, in spite of the unwanted appearances of Harry Bryant and Margo.'

'It doesn't sound as though either of them made a very good impression on you, Jack?'

'You could say that.' Jack pushed away his empty glass. 'She's a perfect madam and I wouldn't trust Bryant as far as I could throw him.'

'And yet, some must, because they buy engine parts from him.'

'True, but I still can't see how he makes enough money to buy *two* boats.'

'Fingers crossed he doesn't then,' said Audrey. 'Can't Laura sway things in Dexter's favour with her father?'

'I doubt it. I get the feeling her paternal feelings are a bit strained these days and her relationship with Charles seems to be going from bad to worse.'

'No love lost there anymore then,' agreed Audrey after hearing of the harsh words said back in Stalham. 'What do you think's happened to turn her against him so suddenly?'

'I don't know, but now's your chance to find out, because here she comes.'

'Hi guys.' In spite of everything, Laura seemed to have bounced back to being her old cheerful self as she joined them at the table. 'Good to see you again, Audrey.' She glanced around at the peaceful setting. 'Well, here we are at last.'

'In spite of a few scares along the way,' added Jack. 'Did Charles ever explain what had given him such a fright at the museum?'

Laura seemed to tense up just at the mention of his name. 'Not to me he didn't, but don't worry, it'll be something of nothing. He's forever looking over his shoulder and imagining things that aren't there.'

'If he *did* imagine it.'

Laura frowned. 'Of course he did, Jack. We're all a bit uptight at the moment anyway, but at least we're spared my father's company this weekend.' She gave a nervous laugh. 'That really would've given Charles something to worry about.'

'And you too, I should think,' said Audrey. 'It must be hard for you, knowing this'll probably be your last trip in *Osprey*.'

'Yes, it is, Audrey, and also for Jim, which is probably why he's not joining us tonight. I don't think he's keen on socialising with the likes of Bryant, so I can understand him preferring a night in Yarmouth to take his mind off it. Ah, here he comes now …' she broke off, as the engineer made his way across the green to join them.

'What can I get you to drink, Jim?' offered Jack after introductions to Audrey.

But he shook his head. 'Thanks anyway, but my taxi will be here shortly.'

'And I can see you're all set for the heady delights of Yarmouth,' commented Laura, noting her engineer's neat appearance and clean change of clothes. 'Is *Osprey* all set for tomorrow?'

'Absolutely. I've tightened the valve-rod glands and stopped that small steam leak.' He paused, self-consciously. 'Laura, do you remember me mentioning an advance?'

'Oh yes, of course.' Laura reached into her bag, extracted an envelope and handed it across. 'There you go, Jim, and a bit extra for all your work … but don't go spending it all at once.'

'Thanks, and I'll try not to …' He stuffed the envelope into his duffel bag at the same time as a car drew into the hotel parking area, '… and here's my taxi … must go.'

'Right, have a good time,' called Laura to his retreating figure.

'A night ashore will do him good,' said Jack, 'even though he didn't seem particularly excited at the prospect.'

Laura nodded. 'Perhaps, after his years in prison, he's just a bit daunted at the thought of crowds.'

'He seemed to be coping well enough this afternoon, but a stretch inside can change a man. Perhaps that's why he feels secure on *Osprey* … his own little world and the only home he's known since being released.'

'Hard to believe someone so decent would ever get on the wrong side of the law,' remarked Audrey. 'I'm just sorry he won't be with us for the meal.'

'Well, I'm not,' said Jack.

Audrey looked a bit shocked. 'But I thought you liked Jim?'

'I do, and it's not personal. It's just that I've been adding up the numbers sitting round the table tonight.'

'Numbers?'

'Yes. If Jim joined us there'd be thirteen having dinner, and the old superstition regarding that number …'

'… means that one of us wouldn't be long for this world,' completed Laura.

'Well, thank goodness we'll only be twelve then,' said Audrey, glad to get off the subject and happy to see other members arriving.

'I never did get to introduce you properly, so this is John and Eileen,' said Laura as Doctor Edwards and his wife joined them at the table. 'You'll remember their boat's called *Patience*, which is certainly apt, knowing all the care John's lavished on her.'

'Which deserves a drink at least,' said Jack, catching the eye of the waitress and ordering another round. With them served, he offered a toast. 'Here's to the wonderful job you've done on her, John.'

'Purely a labour of love,' assured the doctor. 'I've always had a passion for steam boats, but it was hard finding one big enough to sleep on.'

'And you'll be staying on board tonight?'

'Oh, yes ... all part of the boating experience.'

'Which is more than Mum and Charles will be doing,' said Laura, disapprovingly. 'They've got a room in the hotel.'

The doctor nodded. 'Yes, they passed us just now on their way to check in.'

'Oh no! It can't be.'

For a second, Jack struggled to understand the context of Laura's utterance until he followed her gaze to the hotel car park and the dark-blue BMW just pulling in. 'Something wrong, Laura?'

'You could say that.' She shook her head unbelievingly as a tall, attractive-looking man in his mid-fifties climbed out. 'It's only my father.'

* * *

'Well, that was a turn-up for the book,' said Doctor Edwards putting another round of drinks on the table. 'Laura told me her old man definitely wasn't going to be here.'

In the cool of the evening, the foursome had moved inside to the public bar where ancient marshman's tools, old boat blocks and assorted other Broadland memorabilia hung from the walls, adding at least some warmth to an atmosphere that Jack was finding increasingly tense. 'That's what we all thought, John.'

Eileen took a sip of wine. 'I wonder what caused him to change his mind?'

'Or *who*?' Jack was scanning the other members having pre-meal drinks, though not necessarily enjoying themselves. At a nearby table, the Hillbecks had allowed themselves to be cornered by Harry Bryant, who was now endlessly regaling them with stories from his dubious past. 'He's one candidate for sure.'

'We don't *know* that, Jack,' cautioned Audrey, 'but perhaps Laura will be able to tell us.'

'Except we haven't seen her or her father since he arrived,' pointed out Doctor Edwards.

'I've always had the impression that the two of them weren't exactly on the best of terms,' whispered Eileen Edwards, confidentially, to Audrey. 'Apparently, there was a bad falling out several years ago. I'm not sure of the reason, but it seems to have left a permanent rift in their relationship.'

'Laura certainly didn't seem too pleased to see him just now.'

'And I'm not so sure she'll be too thrilled to see *her* either,' added Jack, nodding towards the somewhat shapely figure of Margo just flouncing her way into the bar and taking a corner table well away from the rest.

'No Dexter yet then,' noted Audrey.

'He was still cleaning down his engine when we last saw him,' said Doctor Edwards. 'Reckoned he'd meet us all in the dining room at seven.'

'You've obviously been in *Steambuffs* a while, John,' said Jack. 'Do you know Ralph Lampeter well?'

'Not really. At the few events he's actually deemed to attend, we've found him a bit standoffish. I don't know why. When it comes to steamboats he doesn't actually have much of a clue.'

'Not everyone lives and breathes the subject like you do, John,' soothed Eileen, with an affectionate pat of her husband's well-padded knee.

'Probably felt a bit intimidated amongst all us steamheads,' suggested the doctor. 'That and, perhaps, knowing we're a bit suspicious of his motives for running that charity of his.'

Audrey blinked twice. 'But, surely he should be praised for that, shouldn't he, John?'

'On the face of it, yes, but Ralph has never seemed the type to help anyone but himself. Anyway, you can form your own opinion,' he concluded with a warning nod, 'because here he is.'

All eyes turned to the far end of the bar-room where the man himself was just ducking his head below the low-beamed lintel. Laura followed him in, but already he was heading straight for Margo's table, leaving his daughter to get her own drink.

'He could of at least have said "hello",' muttered Eileen.

'I think he had other things on his mind.' Jack folded his arms. 'I thought Margo was the one who never attended rallies.'

'We've *never* seen her before ...' confirmed Eileen, '... thank goodness.'

'Well, she didn't seem surprised to see Ralph here and they appear to know each other quite well,' observed Audrey as the pair greeted each other with a warm embrace. 'Oh well, that's one in the eye for everyone else, as he didn't even give the rest of you a second glance.'

'Nobody seems that keen for his company anyway,' said Jack, not failing to notice just a little frostiness in the other members' reaction to Ralph's entrance. 'Anyway, here's Laura.'

'Phew, I could have done without him turning up like that,' she sighed, plonking herself down on a stool at their table, gin and tonic in hand, and a weary look on her face. 'But the hotel have kindly squeezed him in for the meal.'

'Bit unexpected though,' said Jack. 'Didn't he give you any warning?'

'None. The first I knew he'd changed his mind was when he just turned up.'

'For what reason?'

'Reckons it was a last-minute decision and didn't want to waste time calling me.' Laura frowned, sceptically. 'I suspect there's more to it than that though. I reckon Bryant's been on to him regarding *Osprey* and Father's come to sort a deal.'

'That won't make Dexter very happy ... or seeing those two together either,' said Jack, nodding to where Ralph and Margo were enjoying a cosy conversation over drinks just delivered from the bar.

Laura turned and gave a withering look. 'Typical.'

'Looks as if they're old friends.'

'From way back, and he's even had the nerve to rearrange my seating plan so he's sitting next to her for the meal.'

'Does your mum know he's here?' asked Audrey.

'Oh yes, and you can imagine the enthusiasm that was greeted with. I'm not sure how either she or Charles will handle the situation ... but we'll soon find out,' she added as a waitress signalled they were ready in the dining room.

They all filed out, conversation perhaps a little muted, and Jack not mentioning that Ralph's addition had put their dining number back to thirteen.

*　　*　　*

As on all these occasions, it took a few minutes for everyone to sort their places at the large round table filling the function room. Finally, Ralph took his seat between Doctor Edwards and Margo, who was already pouring herself another large glass of wine. Next to her, husband Dexter seemed glad to have Jack on his right. Perhaps it was a change in dynamics that prompted Laura to give only the most cursory words of welcome before the first course was served.

With everyone eating, Jack took the opportunity to scan the table. He and Audrey were the only couple not sitting together, though he was sure she was happy between Eileen and Laura who had her mum on her other side. Harry Bryant was again boring Lionel with endless banter, while on his other side, Charles was wisely avoiding eye contact altogether.

'Poor Lionel's drawn the short straw tonight,' whispered Pat who, true to Laura's promise, had been placed next to Jack.

Jack could only agree, and he would have liked to continue chatting to bubbly Pat, who might even know something of Laura's story. Right now, though, he felt his company was more needed by Dexter on his other side, clearly very down and already well into his cups. 'Cheer up, Dexter. It can't be that bad.'

'Can't it?' The ex-mariner pushed away his starter, almost untouched. 'Not from where I'm sitting, Jack.' He nodded towards Ralph, pouring Margo yet another glass of wine. 'I've already told him I'm withdrawing my offer for *Osprey*?'

'*Withdrawing!*' Jack forced himself to lower his voice. 'But what about your proposed trip-boat business?'

'Back on ice ... along with the rest of my life. I need the money for something else now.'

Jack glanced sideways to Margo, laughing as she leaned ever-closer to Ralph. 'You mean to give to your wife?'

'I've got no choice, Jack.'

'Yes, but marital loyalty works both ways, Dexter. You're the one making all the sacrifices while Margo flirts with Ralph right under your nose?'

'She's trying to enlist *his* help as well, Jack. Even letting go of *Pickle* won't solve the problem completely.'

'So, Bryant's having your boat?'

'Yes, we did a deal on the way here.'

'Which will leave you without any boat at all.' Jack shook his head. 'It must be costing you thousands to bail Margo out. For crikey's sake, Dexter, what's the woman done?'

'Who knows?'

'Okay, but what's going on between her and Ralph?'

The waitress arrived with the main course, but Dexter waved his away and instead ordered another whisky. 'There's been something going on between those two for years now.' While absent-mindedly playing with his unused table knife, he cast yet another glance towards Margo, whose inhibitions were disappearing as fast as the wine from her bottle. 'I might be about to lose my boat and my dreams, Jack, but I'm damned if I'll stand by and lose my wife as well ... for all her faults.'

'You mustn't lose either, Dexter. No-one here wants Bryant to get *Osprey*.'

'I think it's too late, Jack. He's already made a good offer for it.'

'What about Helen? Can't she stop the sale?'

'No point even trying if I haven't the money to buy it anyway.'

'But why on earth would Bryant want *two* steamboats? Does the man know what he's taking on?'

'Oh, he knows *exactly* what he's doing ...' Dexter's whisky arrived and he took a good gulp, '... but all I'm concerned about now is keeping my wife out of trouble.'

Jack noticed Dexter's hand tighten around the knife when he said that. Now wasn't the time to press for more details. Across the table, the rest of the group were quietly carrying on their conversations while trying to ignore the tense atmosphere building up around them. Even good food and wine, it seemed, weren't going to paper over the gaping cracks appearing in *Steambuffs'* ranks.

*   *   *

'Okay ... I'll sort something.'

Jack switched off his mobile. It was much later in the evening now, the meal over and he and Audrey outside the hotel preparing to make their farewells.

'Problems, Jack?' Standing nearby, Laura had noticed his brief scowl.

'A slight one, yes. That was Broads Control saying that one of our other launches has gone unserviceable. So now they need mine for tomorrow.'

'But *you* can still be with us?'

'Oh yes ... but boatless.'

Laura shrugged. 'That's no problem. You can come with me in *Osprey*.'

'How will your father feel about that?'

'It doesn't matter, because he won't be on board. He's opted for a night here in the hotel and then plans to drive to How Hill by car in the morning.'

'But he'll miss the best part of the trip.'

'I don't think that will worry him unduly.' She rolled her eyes. 'Reckons that, after his long journey here, he needs to have a lie-in and give his dicky heart a rest.'

'He'd do better to lay off the drink and philandering.'

'Quite, but that's father.' She shrugged. 'Anyway, a good chance for you to handle *Osprey*, Jack.'

'I'll be delighted.'

'Good.' By now, Dexter had staggered out, blinking distractedly in the cool night air. 'Turning in early, Dexter?'

'Too true. I've had enough of everything and everyone for one evening. Goodnight.'

'Poor chap,' commiserated Laura as he lurched away. 'Heart of gold, but that wife of his would drive anyone to drink.'

'Where is she anyway?' asked Audrey.

Laura nodded back to the hotel. 'Still in there. You'd never get the likes of Margo roughing it by sleeping on board so, true to form, she's got herself a soft bed for the night.'

Jack gave a little scoff. 'I wonder whose?'

'I think we can guess, and she won't be sailing to How Hill with the rest of us either.' Laura nodded towards her father's BMW parked close by. 'Apparently, she's hitched herself a lift ... which is probably for the best anyway. Margo doesn't do early mornings, and she'd only delay the rest of us getting away.'

'We're the ones who need to get away now, Jack,' prompted Audrey, 'as I'll need to drive you back here first thing.'

'Right, but I need to go and pay for our meal first.'

'The meal was on me, Jack,' insisted Laura. 'You just settle for your drinks and that'll be fine.' She picked up her own bag, from which came the clink of glass, and grinned mischievously. 'My own left-over wine which, combined with a good book, will get me off to sleep tonight.'

'Very wise.' With Laura gone, Jack returned to the hotel, managed to avoid Harry Bryant still holding forth in the bar and headed straight for the dining-room in search of their waitress. She was nowhere to be seen, but two men remained, still seated at the table and deep in conversation. They were Ralph Lampeter and Charles Seager.

*   *   *

'Shame on you, Jack, eaves-dropping like that.' At this late hour, the road ahead was reasonably quiet as Audrey sped them homewards while listening to Jack's account of the dining room encounter. After her token disapproval, she managed just the briefest of pauses before succumbing to curiosity. 'So, what were those two unlikely chums finding to chat about?'

'Going by the brief snatches I heard from just outside the door, nothing too chummy *or* chatty, actually,' admitted Jack. 'Ralph was sounding pretty intolerant, and saying "You need to get a grip, Seager, and stop imagining

52

things", and Charles was being insistent and saying, "There's nothing wrong with *my* nerves. It was *him*, I tell you".'

'Who do you reckon this "him" was they were talking about?'

'Presumably, the apparition Charles reckoned to have seen at the museum.'

'At least we know now it's a male ghost,' teased Audrey, 'but you didn't hear any more?'

'No, the waitress came back and I had to play the innocent.'

'A pity,' sighed Audrey as she swung them off the main road and onto the narrow lane for home. 'Considering those two are supposed to hate each other, it's amazing they were talking at all.'

'There didn't seem to be too much love lost between them as it was,' agreed Jack, 'but there was something going on between them and it wasn't just about a divorce for Helen.'

'Yes, well, talking of "things going on", Margo and Ralph weren't being very discreet during the meal, were they? I'm amazed poor Dexter puts up with it.'

'He's putting up with more than that,' said Jack, before going on to relate the rest of the evening's strained conversation.

'I don't know which is worse,' sighed Audrey, 'the thought of Bryant getting *Osprey* or Margo taking advantage of Dexter's loyalty. But you say he wouldn't let on why his wife needs so much money?'

'No, because I don't think he knows himself, but it has to be one of two things. Either she's got some sort of medical issue and needs private treatment, or ...' Jack paused, '... she's being blackmailed.'

'Blackmailed!' Audrey swerved momentarily as a barn owl winged its way through their headlights. 'Over what, Jack?'

'Who knows, but let's face it, Margo's certainly no saint.'

'Far from it, and it can't be her infidelity, seeing as she seems quite happy to flaunt her relationship with Ralph in front of all and sundry.'

'Exactly, Aud, so it has to be something more threatening than her reputation. Whatever it is though, she's obviously got in way over her head.'

'And serious enough to have Dexter selling his beloved *Pickle*, withdrawing his bid for *Osprey*, and her trying to soft-talk Ralph Lampeter for what she can get out of him as well.'

Jack shrugged. 'Of course, there are a couple of positive aspects to all this.'

'Which are?'

'With the pair of them loving it up in the hotel, Helen's been presented with her own grounds for divorcing Ralph.'

'Good point, Jack, but what's the other?'

'Me getting a trip in *Osprey* tomorrow.'

'Yes, well, I hardly think that justifies all this immorality, Jack Fellows,' scorned Audrey, 'but time alone with Laura might just get you some extra information.' They were in the village now, drawing up in front of their cottage and Audrey switching off. In the silence she said, 'My own gut feeling is that the sooner this weekend and the rally are over, the better.'

'Yes, but How Hill tomorrow promises to be a good day,' placated Jack, 'so how about you joining me there later for a stroll.'

'... well away from all those *Steambuffs* and their complicated lives,' said Audrey agreeably. 'Yes, I'd love that, Jack, and so will Spike.'

'Right, that's a date then.' They went in and straightway to bed, Audrey looking forward to visiting one of her favourite spots, and Jack, not convinced that the path ahead would be quite so pleasant as the one through How Hill.

*   *   *

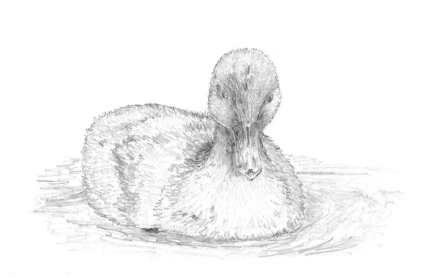

Chapter Six

'Okay, cast off.'

With an acknowledging wave, Jack unhitched *Osprey*'s lines from their mooring posts, threw them onto the steamer's deck and quickly followed them on board. He was still cheesing them down into neat coils when a jangle of bells and a surge of water at the stern announced the engine going ahead. Then, with a cheerful toot from her steam whistle, *Osprey* was gliding past the other steamboats, their own crews busily preparing for departure from Sutton Staithe.

Clear of the moorings, Jack joined Laura in the wheelhouse. She was standing relaxed and focussed at the wheel, clear-eyed and with a look of complete contentment on her face. It wasn't difficult to see why. Ahead, Sutton Broad shone in the early morning sunshine, its surface a mirror of undisturbed tranquillity. On the edge of the nearby reedbeds, a grey heron stood statue-like, patiently scanning the depths for any fish careless enough to cross his path.

'I see old Frank is all set for his breakfast.'

Laura gave a bemused look. 'Frank?'

'Yep, the name given to all herons on the Broads. I'm not sure why. One theory is that it's a corruption of their call.'

'I guess there's some story behind every name unique to the Broads... but I'll certainly listen out for that one.'

'It probably won't sound as sweet as that engine though,' said Jack, cocking an ear below to the reassuring rumble of *Osprey*'s power-plant.

'No, it does sound pretty smooth doesn't it?' Laura cast a glance astern. 'Are the other boats following okay?'

'Yep, the last one's just left the staithe.'

'Good.' She went over to a small scuttle opening down into the boat's machinery space. 'Just a few more revs, Jim.'

'Aye, aye,' came a tired-sounding voice from below.

Jack smiled. 'By the sound of it, your engineer had a good evening in Yarmouth. What time did he arrive back?'

'I'm not sure, actually. I woke around four-ish though and sensed that someone had just come on board, so I assumed it was him.'

'A night on the tiles then. Did he have a good time?'

'He *said* he did when I asked him, though I actually got the impression it hadn't been that much fun.' Laura gave a bemused look. 'Anyway, it hasn't put him off because he's going there again this evening.'

'Hmm. Becoming a bit of a habit. I wonder why?'

'Probably just the lure of bright lights. Actually, it works out well, because Father's sleeping on *Osprey* tonight.'

'How about you? Will you be staying on board with him?'

She smiled. 'No, thank God. An old friend's found out I'm here and invited me to stay the night. We're meeting up for a meal in Norwich first, which will be just like old times.'

'Good for you. It'll give you a break from steamboats.'

'A break from my father and Harry, more like.'

Steaming along, helming *Osprey* around the first of the Ant's many meanders with the varnished spokes of the wheel feeding through her fingers with almost sensual tenderness, Jack thought Laura looked more at ease than at any time since her arrival in Norfolk. He glanced aft to *Pickle* following close astern, the launch's light blue awning still dark with condensation. Beneath it, Dexter was showing little evidence of the previous evening's excess as he helmed *Pickle* resolutely in *Osprey*'s wake, though making no attempt at conversation with Harry Bryant lounging sullenly in the sternsheets. Jack could sense the tension hanging over the boat, as tangible as the funnel smoke lingering in the early morning stillness. 'Oh dear ... not a happy crew in *Pickle*.'

'I can imagine.' Laura shook her head. 'He's dreading handing over *Pickle* to that man as much as I am *Osprey*. Ah well ...' she gave the wheel a tap and stood back, '...come on, Jack, have a go so I can go out and breathe some of this pure Broadland air.'

'Thanks, I'd love to.' Taking the wheel, Jack tried a few gentle inputs, delighting in the honest way the old boat handled. 'She's lovely on the helm, isn't she?'

'Like any well-mannered old lady,' agreed Laura with a smile. 'If you're happy, I'll pop down and get Jim to join me. He could probably do with a breather himself.'

'Right.' Left alone in the wheelhouse, chugging along to the background thump of the engine and the click of its valve-gear, Jack knew he should have been feeling complete contentment. Instead, he found himself mulling over last night's events and what might yet transpire. Was he being overly suspicious about what were probably just strange coincidences? Or was there more to this weekend that he had yet to fathom?

*   *   *

Such thinking was soon cut short by Laura's return to the wheelhouse with Jim. The engineer seemed just a little wary at the sight of the ranger. 'Morning, Jack.'

'Morning, Chief. I hear you enjoyed Yarmouth so much, you're off there again tonight.'

Jim shot Laura an admonishing look as though preferring his evening visits stayed confidential. 'Er ... yes ... thought I might as well make the most of it while I'm here.'

'Doing what?'

'What do you mean?'

'What do you enjoy most there?'

'Oh, you know ... the nightclubs ... what have you.'

He was saved from further questioning by Laura's glance at the wheelhouse clock. 'Time for coffee, I think. How about a cuppa out on deck, Jim?'

The engineer, clearly relieved, headed aft to the saloon. Jack waited until he was out of hearing. 'You're right, his evening ashore seems to have left him up-tight about something. Perhaps he's just worrying about his job situation when *Osprey*'s sold.'

Laura shrugged. 'He might actually be better off. I know Harry Bryant would like to take him on in his workshop.'

'I can understand why. Jim's a skilled engineer, but it's not something *he* wants.'

'It would certainly be a step-down from his present job,' agreed Laura, absent-mindedly stroking the brasswork of the engine room tell-tales. 'We both hate the thought of losing *Osprey* to someone we can't abide.' She seemed to be making an effort to shrug off the prospect. 'That's life, though, Jack. We don't always get the chance to have what we want, do we?'

'No, but that shouldn't stop us trying.' Jack was easing the boat out into mid-stream to pass a slow-moving sailing cruiser, almost becalmed in the still-windless air. 'Surely that's what your father's *New Start* is all about ... giving people a chance?'

'Is it?' She spoke the words with undisguised scepticism. 'A nice thought, Jack, but you obviously don't know my father like I do.'

'Seeing as I've not even exchanged one word with him, I haven't had much opportunity.'

57

'If I were you, I'd keep it that way,' advised Laura. 'Believe me, most of those who have dealings with Father end up loathing him.'

'Margo doesn't seem to.'

'Margo would play up to anyone if she thought there was something in it for her, and wouldn't care who she hurt in the process.' Laura glanced astern to *Pickle*. 'Poor Dexter's looking utterly dejected, and who can wonder. He told me earlier that Margo won't be with him again for tonight's stop at Ludham Bridge.'

'A shame he doesn't at least have the prospect of owning *Osprey* to look forward to.'

'I know,' sympathised Laura. 'Last night before the dinner, I did try and talk Father out of selling it to Bryant, but he didn't even want to discuss it.'

There was a lot this group didn't want to discuss, thought Jack as he eased them around the next meander - visitations by some unknown entity, illicit liaisons, strange boat deals ... and why was Jim Rowston so secretive about his evening ashore?

The man himself had just reappeared with a tray of coffees, their percolated aroma a welcome carrier back to reality. Jack took his mug and and looked out over the bow to where Barton Broad was opening up ahead, its wide expanse sparkling in the rising sun as a slight breeze rippled the surface and filled the sails of river cruisers just getting under way.

Jim stood beside him, gazing at the scene, the weariness in his face and manner somehow dissipating in the natural pleasure of it all. 'This is the sort of place I used to dream of during bleak hours locked in my cell.'

'I hope it comes up to expectations then, Jim.'

'Absolutely. Freedom is such a precious thing, isn't it? Seeing this would make many a man think twice about losing it.'

'Yes, heavenly,' agreed Laura. She took a quick glance at the wheelhouse clock. 'And good progress too.'

In their passage, if not in explanations, thought Jack as they entered the broad.

*   *   *

After crossing Barton, the small flotilla progressed down the narrow Ant, a little steadier now as they met other boats in the confined waterway, many slowing for a better look at these classic craft from another era. As they neared the tiny village of Irstead, Jim decreased speed still further. This gave Laura the opportunity to admire the handsome riverside houses fronting the shoals and, further along behind the public staithe, the typically Broadland parish church of St Michael's whose bells announcing morning service only added to the sense of timelessness this little flotilla was producing.

Leaving Irstead astern, a further mile-and-a-half of winding river had Jack then pointing out a gaunt skeleton windpump and, beyond that, some extensive moorings. 'That's Boardman's Mill with How Hill just ahead.'

Always a popular stopping place, there were already several visiting boats and plenty of people on the shore to take lines as the steamboats eased into the few available slots. As Laura checked all was well with their fendering and Jim went about his engine routines, Jack excused himself to go and meet Audrey, who should have arrived by now and was probably waiting.

Nearing the main staithe, he was happy to see Pat Hillbeck walking ahead before turning right over a small bridge towards Toad Hole Cottage, where the old marshman once lived. 'Good morning, Pat. You seem intent on a mission.'

She spun around, her usual cheerful self. 'Oh, good morning to you, Jack. Lionel's sorting out *Whisper*, so I'm off to check sons Jamie and Sam have arrived okay with our other steam gear.'

'Yes, I forgot you've got your own demo here today. I'm meeting Audrey further up by the main house so I'll walk with you.'

Ambling up the shady incline, Jack was keen to hear more about the Hillbeck's other steam interests.

'The boys are bringing the old sawing unit and our steam traction engine to drive it,' explained Pat, enthusiastically. 'That way How Hill will get their wood sawn and the public will enjoy watching how it was done all those years ago.'

'Sounds as if all your family are involved.'

She nodded, proudly. 'I'm afraid so. Of course, Lionel was the one who started the collection, but I got caught up in the romance of it all and now it's passing to another generation.'

'A bit like Laura and her mum ... or it would be if Ralph passed *Osprey* onto his daughter instead of selling it.'

'Oh, I know. Laura said last night how unhappy she was at the boat going out of the family.' Pat wrinkled her nose. 'Poor lass. *Osprey*'s been the love of her life really, to the extent of showing no interest in settling down and getting married. Not for the want of offers though, I can assure you.'

'Yes, it's such a shame she hasn't found a soul-mate to share her passion for steamboats, but I gather she did fall for someone back in her university days.' Jack knew this was pure speculation on his part, but allowing suspects to *think* you knew more than you did had always worked well back in police days and he was glad to find now it still did with Pat.

'I think there *was* a chap once,' said Pat, frowning, 'but I understand it ended badly. I've never found out what really happened, though I seem to think it was sometime just after she graduated.'

'Whenever, it's a pity because she's a lovely girl.' Jack lowered his voice slightly. 'Not a bit like that father of hers.'

'Yes, Ralph can give the impression of being a bit arrogant,' agreed Pat, 'but you have to understand he's had his own share of problems, what with losing his construction business as well as his wife, and then being diagnosed with that slight heart condition.'

'But then establishing a charity rehabilitating ex-prisoners. *New Start* can't be cheap to run, so where does he get the money?'

'Various government grants backed up by lots of fundraising, I understand,' explained Pat. 'And, of course, some of it has now become self-sustaining, like Harry Bryant's *Heritage Engineering* works.'

'I haven't exactly warmed to Bryant yet,' admitted Jack, 'but I understand he does come up with the goods.'

Pat nodded. 'We've bought several parts from him ourselves. Lionel reckons they're very good and reasonably priced.' They were nearing the top of the track with the grassy slopes of How Hill spreading out to their right. Near the top, a large steam traction engine was already getting up steam. 'That's our beauty and she's only working now because of some parts from *Heritage Engineering*. I know the man's a bit rough around the edges, but *Steambuffs* shouldn't really fault the way he's helped them.' Two young men were rigging a drive belt from the engine to a large sawing rig and, close by, a large pile of logs lay ready for cutting into planks. Already the Hillbeck's collection was drawing fascinated onlookers. 'Good, the lads seem all set to go. Sorry, Jack, nice talking to you, but duty calls.'

'Of course.'

As she headed off, Jack continued up the path to the house itself. He could already see Audrey waiting on a seat with Spike beside her, the collie's tail furiously wagging as he recognised his master.

*   *   *

'Sorry I'm a bit late, Aud, but Pat and I were having a good old mardle.'

'So I could see.' Audrey stood up to receive a welcoming kiss from her husband. 'I hope you found out something.'

'A bit.'

'Fill me in later then.' Audrey was obviously determined to keep this beautiful morning pleasurable. 'There's no rush. It's been lovely just relaxing here in the sun listening to the birds. One thing I did have time to look at though, before I sat down, was that lovely carving of a sailing boat on top of the varnished tree stump over there. It says that was originally an oak tree awarded to Christopher Boardman at the 1936 Berlin Olympics.'

'That's right, the son of the chap who designed and built How Hill, and who won a gold for Britain in one of the sailing events. Each medal winner was given a year-old sapling to take back to their home country to plant as a sign of peace.'

'A nice sentiment, but a pity war broke out three years later,' replied Audrey, cynically.

'Quite.' Jack glanced down at Spike, shuffling impatiently on the end of his lead. 'And *we're* not going to get any peace until this old boy's had his walk. How about a stroll around the Secret Garden?'

'Perfect, and on the way you can tell me all you've found out.'

They set off through the wicket gate and down an enchanting woodland trail where the late morning sun's rays shafted through the branches. As Spike happily zigzagged ahead at the end of his long lead, Jack related what he had learned of Laura's father from Pat Hillbeck.

'Not much we didn't know already, actually,' said Audrey, not particularly impressed.

'No, but it has established a more direct link between *New Start* and Bryant's engineering outfit.'

'Nothing wrong with that is there?' replied Audrey. 'Ralph Lampeter certainly seems a bit full of himself, but he's doing a lot of good for a lot of people.'

'*And* perhaps for himself.'

'What do you mean by that?'

'Oh, just a thought ...' Jack frowned, '... and Laura doesn't seem to harbour any great love for him, going by her reaction when he got here.'

'Well, he did turn up without warning, Jack, and complicated all her carefully laid out plans.'

'At least it's given her the excuse to go off to Norwich this evening to see an old friend. She seems quite excited at the prospect.'

'It'll do her good to have a bit of time to herself away from the hassle of the rally,' agreed Audrey. 'Anyway, here's the Secret Garden, so shorten Spike's lead and let's forget other people and steamboats for a bit and just enjoy a wander.'

Soon they were following a narrow boardwalk that led them contentedly between blossoming flowers, colourful shrubs and lillied pools, an area that had once been rough grazing marsh, but was now home to numerous exotic and foreign horticultural species. Before long, they were stopping for a rather snug sit on "Molly's Chair", a wood framed, reed-lined seat in the shade of what the sign described as a Japanese Katsura tree. 'So peaceful and tranquil,' said Audrey quietly, stretching her legs with a sigh. 'Let's hope some of your *Steambuffs* lot come down here and soothe their troubled souls.'

Jack shook his head, regretfully. 'Sadly, I think it might take a bit more than this to sort some of them.'

'Poor Dexter for one,' agreed Audrey. 'Do you really think his wife *is* being blackmailed?'

'Can't think why else she'd be that desperate for money.'

'So, why doesn't she go to the police?'

'Usually, it's the fear of a scandal but, knowing Margo, I'd bet it's something illegal she's done herself.'

'Such as?'

'I'm not sure, but it could well be connected to this mysterious antique trading she seems to be involved with. Whatever, someone's putting pressure on her and I bet it's the mystery figure who scared her so much at *ArtVu*.'

'And if that's the same person who spooked Laura and Seager, then it must all be connected. That's pretty frightening, Jack.'

'And mystifying, but something I need to figure out.'

'Oh *please* don't get involved,' pleaded Audrey. 'They'll all be gone in a couple of days, so why don't you, just for once, turn a blind eye. Things might not erupt until after the rally anyway and, who knows, it could all be something of nothing in the end.'

'Like hoping dark clouds on the horizon won't bring rain,' scoffed Jack, 'except they usually do.'

'Well, there are no "dark clouds" here right now, Jack, so let's just enjoy the healing effect of this beautiful garden while we can.'

But Spike, until now lying contentedly at their feet, suddenly raised his head as, from somewhere out of sight further down the boardwalk, there came the harsh raised voice of an angry female.

Jack recognised it straight away. 'That's Margo Berrington.'

'And she doesn't sound too happy.' Audrey stood up to retrace their steps. 'Come on, Jack, let's go back.'

'Not when there's the chance of eavesdropping, I won't.' Jack put a restraining hand on his wife's shoulder and a calming one on Spike. 'Come on, let's get closer.'

'Jack, we can't,' whispered Audrey.

'Yes we can.' Taking Spike's lead, Jack led them stealthily in the direction of the voice.

*   *   *

Audrey followed, still unhappy to be intruding, but, in all honesty, as curious as her husband to find out just what was going on. Putting a finger to his lips, Jack pulled her into the cover of some nearby ferns where Spike, conscious as ever as to what was required of him, lay down full-stretch without so much as a grunt. Just as well, because they were as close as they could get to the secluded dell from which Margo's words were becoming ever-angrier.

'I'm only asking for a loan, for God's sake.'

'But for a considerable one.'

It wasn't difficult to identify the urbane voice of the other party. 'That's Ralph Lampeter,' whispered Audrey, and Jack nodded back.

'It's a matter of life or death, Ralph,' beseeched Margo in an even higher octave.

'Exactly, my dear. *Your* life or *your* death.' Ralph's voice remained the same, be it totally unsympathetic. 'I'm strapped myself at the moment, so there's no way I can help you.'

'Don't give me that rubbish.' Margo's anger was now partially dissolved in sobs. 'Your sort are never short of cash.'

'They are when people like you don't hand over the earnings. Don't go asking for money when you still owe me for our last transaction.'

'Look, I promise I'll settle up with you when I can, but until then, please, *please* help me, Ralph. I beg you. I'm desperate and money's the only way out of this nightmare.'

'You created it, so you sort it.'

'Damn you, Ralph!' fired back Margo. 'Just remember, if I can't pay up and the truth comes out, you'll be in it up to your neck too. I'll make bloody sure you won't get off scot-free. I thought we had something, but I know now I mean nothing and you've just been using me.'

'I think the arrangement's benefitted us both, don't you?'

'All right, so I did something stupid a long time ago, but I never thought it would come back to haunt me like this.' Margo seemed to be trying to pull herself together. 'Well, if you won't help me financially, then how about a bit

63

of muscle? You know who it is, so surely you could put a bit of pressure where it hurts.'

'What, and risk it backfiring on me?' Ralph gave an audible scoff. 'Not likely. You're on your own this time, Margo dear. If you involve me, you'll only dig a deeper hole for yourself.'

'And it'll be worth every spadeful.' There was now a steely edge to Margo's tone. 'If I go down, I'll sure as hell take you with me.'

There were just a few seconds of silence, Ralph clearly weighing his options and Jack and Audrey holding their breath for fear of being heard. Finally he said, 'All right, you take my car back to Stalham now, drive home in yours, and come and see me in *Osprey* at Ludham Bridge tonight.'

'You'll be alone?'

'Yes. Laura sent me a text to say she's going into Norwich to see a friend and that Rowston's off to Yarmouth again, so it'll be quite safe as long as you don't let on to that husband of yours.'

'Don't worry, he's kipping on *Pickle* tonight, but knows I'm going back to our flat this afternoon and sleeping there.'

'Right, well come back at midnight and no-one will know.'

'Okay.' Margo allowed her voice just to soften a shade. 'You won't regret this, Ralph. As you know from last night, I can be awfully grateful when I feel like it.'

'When you *need* to be, more like. Now you just clear off and I'll see you at midnight.'

Jack made sure both Audrey and Spike stayed silent and hidden until both pairs of departing footsteps were well clear.

*   *   *

'Well, it seems as if Margo Berrington is quite capable of trying a bit of blackmail of her own,' said a disgusted Audrey as she, Jack and Spike strolled down the wide sloping grassy expanse to the river.

'It certainly looks that way.' It was well past midday now and they were nearing the staithe. Below them, the River Ant, shimmering in the afternoon sun, wound its eternal way south-westwards through the marshes to join the distant River Bure. Soon, the steamboats would be following it downstream, but Jack's thoughts were still musing over all they'd heard back there in the Secret Garden. 'It's one thing to talk men out of their money, Aud, but this is turning out a whole lot more sinister. Margo's talking "life or death", and probably has good reason to be scared.'

64

'Perhaps it's Ralph himself. He said she owed him money.'

'Doubtful, but I'd dearly like to know more about those "transactions" he was talking about. Whatever they are, you can be sure they're not legitimate. One thing it did confirm though, is that Ralph and Margo's connection goes way back.'

'And not just in the bedroom either,' said Audrey. 'Honestly, Jack, this whole business is pretty sordid. How about this midnight tryst on *Osprey* that they arranged? Are you going to warn Dexter about that?'

'Part of me feels I should, but the other tells me it might be something he'd rather not know. Dear old Dexter's a bit head-in-the-sand when it comes to Margo's infidelity, so what would it achieve? One thing that was significant though, was Ralph knowing who it is was threatening Margo. I wonder why and how?'

'She probably just told him.'

'I'm sure she did, but I still got the impression it was definitely someone they both knew.'

'Could it be Jim Rowston then? We know he's handled drugs before. Perhaps he still does, Ralph and Margo are involved, and she's somehow got the wrong side of him.' Audrey raised knowing eyebrows. 'That could also explain Jim's evening trips to Yarmouth, Jack ... a seaport with ships coming and going and who-knows-what?'

'A possibility I suppose,' acknowledged Jack, reluctantly, 'though Jim didn't arrive with *Osprey* until *after* Margo's scare at *ArtVu*. That's not to say he couldn't have slipped here earlier though, and his Yarmouth trips do seem rather out of character. Either he's formed a sudden addiction to Crazy Golf or there's something fishy going on there.'

'I think there's a lot that's "fishy" about this rally, Jack,' groaned Audrey. 'Thank goodness it'll be all over tomorrow. The sooner it's ended and everyone, including you, goes back to their old lives, the better.'

'It's *how* it ends that worries me,' said Jack, frowning as they arrived back on the staithe. 'Anyway, the boats look all steamed and ready to go. Can you collect me this evening from Ludham Bridge?'

'Of course. I'll come about seven after giving Spike his evening walk. The more distance between you and *Steambuffs*, the happier I'll be.'

'Now who's painting devils?' chided Jack. 'Anyway, seven will be good and perhaps give me a chance to glean a bit more info from some of the others.'

'Just you be careful, Jack.' Audrey glanced to where *Osprey* lay ready for the off. Rather more disconcertingly, Ralph was already on board and leaning casually over the boat's for'ard guardrail. She pulled Jack and Spike to a halt.

'I don't want to face that man now, so I'll say "cheerio" here and see you later.'

'Understood, love. Drive carefully.'

Laura broke off from talking to Jim on the quay as the ranger joined them. 'Right, Jack, we're all set. Anything we need to know about Ludham Bridge?'

'Only that it's a popular place for boats to stop, so expect it to be busy. I doubt there'll be enough free space for us to moor together, but the tide'll be flooding as we get there, so we'll be able to head straight into any slot available without having to turn.'

'Sound's good.' Laura turned back to her engineer. 'Probably best if you stay manning the engine room for the whole trip, Jim. I might have to go astern in a hurry.'

'No problem. Will your father be handling the lines?'

'Why not? He's quick to play the invalid when it suits him, but a bit of deckwork won't do him any harm.'

Jack grinned and glanced further up the quay to where Dexter was single-handedly preparing for departure. 'Where's Bryant?'

Laura nodded back to *Osprey*. 'Down in our saloon for this leg and already knocking back the gin. Apparently, he wants to discuss something with Father.'

'I can guess what.'

'And you'd probably be right. He'll need to keep his hands to himself though if he doesn't want me to chuck him overboard.'

'Not something I'd want to miss,' said Jack, laughing, 'but probably best if I go and keep Dexter company in *Pickle*.'

'He'll like that.'

And so will I if I learn a bit more, thought Jack as he made his way up the quay. He glanced back in time to see Lampeter distastefully unhitching *Osprey*'s mooring lines. Thinking metaphorically, it probably wasn't the first time those hands had been dirtied.

How, why and when, was something he still needed to find out.

*   *   *

'Good ... underway at last,' sighed Dexter as he edged *Pickle* away from How Hill staithe along with the rest of the steamboats. A slight increase on the main steam valve to increase revs and then they were clearing the narrow moorings and maintaining station on *Osprey* just ahead.

Coiling the headrope as they steamed past Turf Fen Mill, Jack paused to savour the reassuring click and hiss of the small open compound. 'Ah, that's how all engines should sound.'

'Too true. You can't beat that old technology.' Dexter glanced astern to check the other boats were duly following before nodding to the varnished bench-seat up in *Pickle*'s bow. 'Sit yourself down and relax, Jack.'

'Thanks, Skipper, don't mind if I do.' Still in the lunch hour, the River Ant was comparatively quiet, save for the gentle swish of their own passage and the song of warblers hidden in the reedbeds. Jack leaned against the back cushion and breathed in the river air. 'This is certainly the life.'

'Yes, but one I probably won't be enjoying for much longer,' sighed Dexter, his eyes fixed longingly on *Osprey* ahead. 'No doubt Lampeter and Bryant are already down in the saloon toasting their deal and having a good laugh at my expense.'

Jack turned to face him. 'Then stop giving them the ammunition, Dexter. Stand up to Margo and tell her she's making a fool of you, and that you're not putting up with it any longer. You can't just sit back while she flirts with Ralph in front of everyone. You need to take the initiative and put an end to it once and for all.'

'I know, Jack.' The fresh morning air seemed to have cleared away the effects of last night's bender and with it, some of his personal inhibitions. 'The truth is, I fell for her knowing all her weaknesses, but what I didn't reckon on were all those prowling wolves ready to take advantage.'

'Like Ralph Lampeter?'

'Exactly. I try to ignore it, but even I'm reaching the end of my tether.'

'Don't let him get to you.' Jack leaned across and put a steadying hand on the skipper's broad shoulders. 'The man's not worth it. But you were right about him and Margo having some sort of business relationship.'

Dexter cast a suspicious glance. 'How do you know that?'

'Don't ask. The important thing is I do, along with the fact that she owes him money?'

'I didn't know that.'

'And, if she gets her way, she'll soon owe him more.' It was cards on table time. 'I think we both know why she's suddenly so desperate for money, don't we Dexter? She's being blackmailed, isn't she?'

Dexter rubbed a weary hand across his face before simply nodding. 'You're right, Jack. Unless we pay up, it's curtains for everything, but what can I do?'

'Go to the police.'

'I can't if I want to keep Margo out of jail.'

'Why, what did she do?'

'She won't say.'

'Or who the blackmailer is?'

'No, but it has to be the mystery figure who frightened her at the gallery.'

'Whoever it is, Dexter, they have to be dealt with through the law. Would you like me to make a few discreet enquiries?'

But, again, Dexter shook his head. 'No way, Jack. I can't risk things going wrong for Margo. The way I understand it, if she wants to stay safe, she has to come up with the money. But we should have enough soon, because I'm closing the deal for *Pickle* with Bryant tonight, and Margo reckons she's set to get more.'

Jack held back from telling this cheated husband he knew how. If Dexter had wind of Margo's midnight tryst on *Osprey* he could well do something they'd all regret. It was time to change this subject and try for more clarity on another. 'Bryant and Jim Rowston, Dexter ... has there been much previous connection between those two?'

'Only when Jim was renovating *Osprey* and needed parts. Why?'

'Oh, just that Jim told me he had no intention of working for him.'

'He might have no choice.' The skipper paused to helm them around yet another of the Ant's meanders. 'Getting another job won't be that easy with his record.'

'Perhaps that's why he's making the most of this weekend then with evening jaunts to Great Yarmouth. Any idea what they're about?'

'Just a change of scene, probably.' Dexter smiled. 'Anyway, he must have had a good time, because he didn't get back until midnight.'

'More like dawn, according to Laura.'

'No, it had to be midnight, Jack. I couldn't sleep with so much turning over in my mind. In the end, I got up and went for a walk down the staithe. I'd just got to the end when I saw someone going on board *Osprey*. I remember looking at my watch and it was just after twelve.'

'And you're sure it was Jim?'

'I couldn't swear to it. It was pitch dark, but I'd just seen a car swing into the car park, so I assumed it was him arriving back by taxi.'

'And he stayed on board?'

'Not sure of that either, but I did hear the car move off again.'

'What, *immediately*?'

'Not really. It must have been after about fifteen minutes.'

'Hmm. Laura did say she was half-asleep when she sensed someone coming back on board, so perhaps she simply got the time wrong.' The remains of Neaves Mill were just coming into sight now, marking the last big curve of the river before Ludham Bridge. Jack was glad to see the outflow from the pump drifting upriver. 'Tide's turned, Dexter. It'll be good for mooring up.'

'I'd better make the most of it then,' said Dexter, sadly. 'I love the challenge of manoeuvring and bringing her alongside, but not something I'll be doing for much longer.'

Jack could feel for the man. 'I know it's not easy, Dexter, but just take things as they come and don't do anything you'd regret.'

'I've got so many regrets, Jack, one more wouldn't make much difference.'

Jack would have liked to help the man more, but Ludham Bridge was in sight now and they'd soon be mooring. As he got their lines ready, he just wished life could be as straightforward as boats.

*　　*　　*

As planned, the already flooding tide had allowed all the boats to head straight into whatever mooring slots were still available, *Osprey* grabbing the first on the upriver end of the east bank while *Whisper* and *Patience* continued further down towards the bridge. As *Sunbeam* chose a quiet spot on the opposite bank, Jack tactfully directed *Pickle* into a space as far from *Osprey* as possible and made fast their lines. After checking the fenders were doing their job, he glanced back up the moorings. 'She'll be safe enough here, Dexter. I'll just go and check that Laura's okay with *Osprey*.'

He found her already ashore with Jim, making fast their lines, but no Ralph. 'What happened to your deckhand?'

She rolled her eyes. 'Too much en route booze, I suspect. He did stick his head out long enough to complain I'd moored too far from the bridge, even though I did point out it was to make sure he had a good night's sleep away from the road and traffic.'

'But he's okay with you being in Norwich tonight?'

'Oh, yes. He seemed quite pleased to be having the boat to himself.'

'So, what time are you leaving?'

'I've booked a taxi for six-thirty,' she nodded towards the engineer just hopping back aboard and disappearing into his engine-room, 'and Jim's heading off for Yarmouth about the same time.'

'Still no idea why?'

'No, but he's young and fancy-free, so perhaps he's got a date.'

'How about the other crews?'

'Going their different ways. Harry Bryant's booked a room at the pub just up the road, but before that he's finalising things with Dexter for *Pickle*. Lionel and Pat are leaving *Whisper* there by the bridge and being transported home again by one of their sons. Doc Edwards and Eileen are, as usual, sleeping onboard *Patience*, and Mum and Seager are planning to walk down the riverbank to the old abbey near here before it gets dark.'

'That'll be Saint Benet's,' said Jack. 'They'll enjoy that. And then, are they sleeping on *Sunbeam* tonight?'

'Afraid not. I think they were a bit spoiled by last night's hotel, so they've got themselves a room at the local as well. Dexter has promised to keep an eye on *Sunbeam* for them ...' Laura gave a cynical smile, '... though the poor chap would probably do better keeping an eye on his wife. Thank goodness she's going home to their flat tonight and staying well clear of here.'

'Yes indeed.' Not wanting to dwell on the subject, Jack quickly changed tack. 'Anyway, how about tomorrow's programme?'

'We all head back to Stalham. Apparently, Harry's going in *Pickle* to get checked out, so it won't be a happy final trip for Dexter.'

'It'll be good to make an early start though,' advised Jack, indicating the river's strengthening flood. 'The tide'll be making again at five in the morning, so I recommend we get away at seven and avoid the scramble later.'

'A wise move I'm sure, though I won't promise Father will be up by then.'

'Where's he now?'

'Still onboard drinking with Harry. Not the best thing for his heart, but at least it keeps that awful man well away from me.'

Jack grinned and then nodded down the quay. 'I'll go now and warn Doc Edwards about tomorrow's early start. If I don't see you before you go, have a good evening.'

'Thanks, Jack, I'm really looking forward to it.'

*　　*　　*

Doctor Edwards was busy cleaning down his boat when Jack joined him hard by the bridge. Not that *Patience* looked as though she needed much attention, the sleek old umpire's launch appearing as immaculate as always.

'You look after her well, John.'

The doctor paused from buffing one of the bronze fairleads. 'I certainly try. She's a hundred and twenty years old so she deserves a bit of pampering.'

'Wish I got half as much,' joked his wife, Eileen, emerging from the cabin with a tray of mugs. She handed one to Jack. 'Here, I expect you're ready for a cuppa. Come on board and relax.'

'Thanks.' Jack settled himself onto one of the cockpit side seats and glanced up at the bridge above them. 'A pity you ended up having to moor so close to the road. You sure you won't be bothered by all that traffic noise?'

'John might be,' answered Eileen. 'He got used to sleeping with one eye open when he was on night duty, but I sleep through anything.'

'And she's not joking, Jack. I climbed back into bed after delivering twins once, and she hadn't even realised I'd gone!' He gave his wife a loving grin. 'Sleeps like a log ... lucky for her.'

'Well, hopefully all that's behind you now. You've certainly earned your retirement ...' Jack glanced around at the surrounding marshland, '... and you couldn't have picked a better place to enjoy it than cruising these waters in *Patience*. Good for *Steambuffs* too, having their own medic along, just in case.'

'They're a pretty fit lot,' assured the doctor, 'so, apart from the odd burn and scald, they don't call on my expertise very often.'

'How about Ralph though? He has a slight heart condition doesn't he ... or shouldn't I ask that?'

'No, that's fine, because he's not my patient and he's never even discussed it with me,' Doctor Edwards replied without compunction. 'Actually, he's made it quite clear he has little time for the medical profession and prefers homeopathic treatments.'

'Ah well, saves the NHS some money,' said Jack, smirking. 'Anyway, he seems ever-ready to use it as an excuse to lie in each morning.'

'That's because he's hung-over, more like,' chipped in Eileen, scathingly. 'If he really wanted to care for his condition, he'd drink less.'

'And stick to tea,' agreed Jack, raising his mug. He paused because Laura was just walking by to meet her taxi. She smiled and waved, transformed now from outdoor girl by smart trousers, lightweight linen jacket and a long silky scarf. An overnight bag was slung casually over her shoulder and, even at that distance, there drifted over the aroma of some expensive perfume.

'Doesn't she look lovely,' said Eileen, returning the wave with a knowing smile. 'It'll be nice for her to visit old haunts with her friend while she's in the area.'

'And escape from that father of hers,' added her husband.

Jack nodded, knowing that Ralph Lampeter was doubtless just as pleased to be having *Osprey* to himself for his midnight tryst with Margo. Up on the road, Laura's taxi had just pulled in and was soon winging her back over the bridge for Norwich.

Jack made his thanks and farewells to John and Eileen, before he too headed to the lay-by for his own pickup by Audrey, the thought of an evening at home, well away from *Steambuffs*, a surprisingly enticing one. Much as he liked many of their members and the beautiful boats they operated, he couldn't help feeling this weekend was heading for a showdown.

'Penny for your thoughts,' said Audrey as she handed Jack his whisky.

'What? ... oh, just thinking about things, Aud.' Relaxed in his favourite armchair with a well-walked Spike lying close by, Jack savoured the first swig from the tumbler. 'Ah, lovely. This'll help me sleep.'

'After a day in the fresh air trying to keep everybody happy, I wouldn't have thought you'd take much rocking tonight anyway.'

'Ah well, you know me, Aud ... always trying to fit the jigsaw of life together.' He shrugged. 'But why should I worry? By this time tomorrow, *Steambuffs* will have finished their rally and be hauling out at Stalham.'

'Exactly, Jack, but it's a shame, because you were really looking forward to this assignment. Now you sound relieved it's almost over.'

'In some ways I am ... or at least I will be if this weekend manages to end without tears.'

'I think you mean if it *only* ends in tears,' laughed Audrey. 'You really would think steamboat owners would be happy like-minded folk, enjoying a weekend together, but I've never known such animosity between a group of people in my life.'

'Some of them certainly seem to be harbouring dark secrets,' admitted Jack, 'and there's one aspect I'm particularly unhappy about.'

'Which is?'

Jack shook his head. 'I can't say, Aud, or at least not until I have more facts. Probably just my old way of seeing trouble ever-lurking, but I hope like hell I'm wrong.'

'Sadly, you rarely are.' Audrey put down her drink and placed a loving hand on her husband's arm. 'But forget all that now and just focus on getting them back in one piece.'

'I'll try.' Jack glanced at the clock on the mantelpiece and stood up. 'Anyway, crack-of-dawn start tomorrow, Aud, so time for bed.'

'Why so early, for goodness' sake?'

'Because some of those cruisers will be making the most of the flood tide for a quick getaway upriver. We've got this far without any knocks and I don't want them bashing our vintage steamboats.' Jack swigged back the last of his drink. 'Sorry, love, but I'll need you to drive me there for six-thirty.'

'Fine by me. The sooner you start, the sooner you'll finish and get back to normal life.'

'Depends what you mean by "normal",' said Jack as he went off to bed.

*   *   *

Chapter Seven

'Remember what I told you,' warned Audrey next morning as she dropped her husband off at Ludham Bridge.

'Of course.' Jack grabbed his bag off the back seat. 'Thanks for the lift, Aud. I'll call you from Stalham when I need the pickup.'

With Audrey speeding back to home and breakfast, Jack cast an eye down to the river, already flowing steadily upstream through the bridge's narrow span. He was about to wander down onto the staithe when a taxi breasted the bridge, pulled in and out jumped Laura.

'Morning, Jack.' This was the old Laura, back in jeans, sweatshirt and trainers. 'And a beautiful one it is.'

'Idyllic.' Jack nodded back down the road towards Norwich. 'How was your evening?'

'Absolutely lovely, thanks ... ' she paused to scan the encircling marshes where a veneer of mist lay veil-like over dykes and reedbeds ' ... but this takes some beating ...' she gave a little shiver, ' ... even if it is a bit chilly.'

'A hot cup of coffee will put that right.' Jack nodded towards the staithe. 'Come on, I'll walk with you to *Osprey*.'

They made their way up the moorings, past *Whisper*, still awaiting the arrival of the Hillbecks, and *Patience* where the ever-fussy Doctor Edwards was already taking advantage of the condensation to wipe down his boat. From the cabin floated the enticing smell of frying bacon as wife Eileen tended her husband's inner needs.

Not so domestically pampered though was Dexter Berrington, alone on *Pickle* and so intent on engine routines that he seemed almost startled by Jack and Laura's morning greeting.

'Oh ... sorry ...' he paused from filling the oil boxes, his hair still tousled and a heaviness about his eyes, '... miles away.'

'Early start for us all,' excused Jack. He tapped the thermos flask in his bag. 'See you soon for a warming coffee.'

'I'll look forward to that.'

'I got the impression he hadn't had much sleep,' whispered Laura as they continued up the staithe, 'but at least he's flashed up his boiler, which is more than Father's managed.' She was looking ahead to the far end of the staithe where *Osprey* lay still and silent, with not a wisp of smoke from her tall funnel.

'Did you really expect it?'

'Not really, but I was hoping Jim might be back and have got things going.' They were alongside the big steamer now with still no hint of movement within. Laura swung her bag on board. 'I suppose I'd better go and spoil the old devil with a morning cuppa.'

'Good luck.'

Jack left her climbing aboard, but had only taken a few steps back down the moorings when she reappeared on deck, her voice high-pitched and edged with near-hysteria. 'Jack ... Jack!'

He wheeled around to see her waving frantically from the boat's afterdeck. 'What's the matter?'

'Please ... come back ... something's happened.'

As curious heads appeared from adjacent cruisers, Jack sprinted back, arriving to find her leaning on *Osprey*'s guardrail, ashen-faced and shaking.

'Laura ...' he leaned across and gripped her arm, '... what's wrong?'

'It's ... it's Father,' she stammered through quivering lips while casting shocked eyes towards the saloon. 'I think ... I think he's dead.'

*   *   *

'Go and get Doc Edwards ...' Jack ordered, ' ... *now*, Laura!'

As she ran down the staithe, the ranger swung himself on board *Osprey*. The saloon doors had been left wide open from Laura's panic-stricken flight. He jumped the two steps into its wood panelled interior where Ralph Lampeter lay slumped in one of the leather chairs, head back, mouth open, eyes staring, bare-footed but fully clothed. Jack felt for any signs of life but found none.

More footsteps sounded on the deck outside followed by Doctor Edwards in the saloon doorway, somewhat breathless, but professionally calm. He said nothing, went straight to Ralph, felt for a pulse, raised one eyelid, straightened up and shook his head.

Laura reappeared, eyes questioning and with Dexter close behind her. Jack stopped her coming closer. 'Sorry, Laura, but he's gone.'

'Oh God.' She put a shaking hand to her mouth.

'Look after her, Dexter. I'll be right with you.'

'Of course.'

As Dexter led the sobbing Laura back out on deck, Jack turned to Doctor

Edwards. 'Well, John?'

'Looks like a heart attack, but that'll be for a pathologist to confirm.' He pulled out his mobile phone. 'I'll call the police.'

'Okay, and I'll go and make sure Laura's okay.'

He found her still onboard, up in the bows with Dexter and as far from the saloon as possible. When Jack joined them she turned, eyes red and staring. 'It was his heart, wasn't it?' She wiped away the rolling tears. 'If only I'd taken his condition more seriously, but I really thought he was putting it on most of the time. I shouldn't have left him last night and gone off enjoying ...'

'No.' Jack stopped her right there. 'Don't go beating yourself up over this, Laura. It looks to have happened just before he went to bed and been very quick. He didn't even have time to call for help on his mobile. Even if you'd been here, there was probably nothing you could have done.' Down on the staithe, people were already gathering, aware that some drama was taking place. On the other bank, in *Sunbeam*, figures were moving. 'It looks like your mum and Charles have just arrived. Let Dexter take you over there and help you break the news while I check the police are on their way.'

Laura looked up, startled. '*Police?*'

'It's procedure, Laura. All sudden deaths are reported. You'll probably have to make a statement later, but leave me to handle things for now. You go with Dexter and let your mum know what's happened. You'll be a comfort to each other after having such a shock.'

They went off, leaving Jack to usher away the onlookers before returning to the saloon. 'The police are on their way,' said Doctor Edwards, putting away his mobile. 'Shouldn't be long.'

'Good.' Knowing he too would have to explain the circumstances, Jack now took time to study this scene of death.

Ralph Lampeter's fine features were already showing a wax-like appearance. 'Any estimate for time-of-death, John?'

'I'd say a good six hours ago at least.' The doctor checked his watch. 'Probably around midnight. Looks like he was just off to bed.'

'But was enjoying a nightcap first,' said Jack, sniffing the half-drunk tumbler of Scotch on the small table between the two easy chairs. 'And not alone either,' he added, noting the wineglass next to it, empty save for its dregs. He glanced back to the corpse. 'Okay if I cover him up?'

'Yes, of course.'

Leaving the saloon, Jack went for'ard to the sleeping cabin and pulled a blanket off the narrow berth. Ralph's washbag and other accessories lay about, but the bunk itself had clearly not been slept in. Back in the saloon, he covered over the corpse, stood back and once more studied the scene. Then he went over to the galley counter where the open bottle of Scotch still stood on the varnished surface.

'You look puzzled, Jack,' said Doctor Edwards. 'Seen something?'

'It's what I haven't seen, actually,' replied Jack, glancing around the rest of the bar, the bottles lining the cupboard behind, the neat rows of glasses hanging in their holders above. 'Mmm, now that's curious as well.'

'What is?'

'Oh, just a couple of things. Something that shouldn't be here and is, and something that should be and isn't.'

'Funny you should be a bit suspicious,' confided Doctor Edwards warily, 'because I saw something a bit odd myself last night.' He paused as though reluctant to cast any aspersions. 'You were right in predicting I might not sleep that well. I dropped off okay, but later I was woken by the noise of someone running down the moorings, a car engine starting right there on the staithe next to *Patience,* and then the thing roaring away as though all the hounds in hell were after it.'

'When was this, John?'

'Just after midnight. I checked it on the boat clock.'

'But you don't know who it was?'

'I know whose *car* it was, because I stuck my head out of the hatch to see what was going on and just caught sight off it speeding back onto the road. It was Margo Berrington's.'

'You sure of that?'

'Absolutely. I'd know that flashy sports-job anywhere.'

'Hmm. You'll need to mention this in any statement the police ask you to give ... and here they are,' he added glancing towards the bridge where a police car had just pulled onto the staithe. 'Can I leave you to handle things, John, while I go and check Laura and her mum are okay?'

'Yes, of course.'

Jack went off, meeting the lone constable on the pathway, giving the briefest of situation reports and directing him to *Osprey.* Then he crossed the bridge and made his way down the opposite bank.

*   *   *

He found Laura on board *Sunbeam* being comforted by her mother and Charles. 'I'm sorry this has happened, Helen, but glad you're here.'

'Planned an early start anyway,' said Seager. 'Didn't expect to find this mess when we arrived, though.'

Jack turned to Laura. 'A policeman will probably be coming to take your statement shortly.'

She shook her head and dried her eyes. 'There's not much I'll be able to tell him.'

'With Ralph's heart condition, he obviously died from natural causes,' said Helen. 'If he'd kept off the drink, he might have lived longer.'

'Were either of you having a drink with him last night?'

'No we certainly weren't. Why would we want to do that?'

'Just that I knew you had certain issues you needed to thrash out.'

'You mean divorce,' broke in Seager. 'We'd already tried to make him see reason and got nowhere ...' he threw Jack a hostile look, '... not that it's any business of yours, Fellows.'

'No, but it could well be the police's, and *they* might want to know where you were last night.'

'If you're implying *we* had something to do with my husband's death,' said an aggrieved Helen, 'I can assure you that at midnight we were both tucked up in bed at the pub.'

'Who said anything about midnight, Helen?'

'Well, I just assumed ... as Laura told me he was still fully-clothed ... he ...'

'... probably popped his clogs sometime then,' broke in Seager, causing Laura to take a sharp intake of breath at the man's lack of subtlety.

'Certainly the preliminary medical evidence indicates that,' said Jack, 'but everything's open until the final verdict. I'm going back to *Osprey* now and suggest you all stay here for the moment.'

On his way back, Jack noticed Dexter close by the bridge talking to Jim Rowston and Harry Bryant. Was it his imagination, or were those last two both casting nervous glances at the police car parked close by?

*   *   *

Back in *Osprey*'s saloon, the young PC was writing in his pocketbook. 'So, Doctor, you reckon a coronary sometime around midnight?'

'That's right. He had a history of heart trouble for which he was taking some form of herbal remedy.'

'Is there any of it on board?'

'I'll go and look,' offered Jack, and soon returned carrying a small plastic bottle.

'Hmm, *digitalis*,' read John Edwards from the label. 'You don't see that very often these days.'

The PC's eyebrows rose. 'You mean it's not a recognised treatment?'

'Not any more. It used to be prescribed as an antiarrhythmic to control heart-rate, but it derives from the foxglove plant, which itself is a pretty toxic agent.' The doctor turned the bottle over in his hand. 'It doesn't say who dispensed it.'

'His daughter might know,' suggested Jack, 'and she's the one who first discovered her father's body.'

'I'll need a statement from her then,' said the PC, 'and from you too, please, Doctor ...'

'... Edwards. No problem, but right now I've got a boat raising steam and only my wife on board so ...'

'Of course, I'll call the coroner, and you get going.'

'Not quite the way any of us expected the rally to end,' commented John Edwards as Jack saw him ashore. 'Eileen and I will go and pay our condolences to Helen and Laura and then slide quietly off.'

But it was going to be difficult to do anything quietly now, thought Jack, as he watched the doctor make his way back down a staithe rapidly coming alive with boats and holidaymakers.

Back in the saloon, the PC had just ended a call on his mobile. 'Coroner's department reckon it'll be an hour before they can get here.'

'Probably a good thing,' said Jack. 'I think it would be best to get this boat shifted to the other side of the bridge away from public gaze. There's a boatyard there with easier access for the coroner's vehicle as well.'

'Good idea. Can you organise that, sir?'

'No problem but, before we go, can I get you to take the contents of that tumbler for analysis.' The PC's eyes rose momentarily at this seeming intrusion into police business, only to nod acceptance once Jack had explained his own years in the Met and Scotland Yard. 'Also bag that wineglass next to it to check for prints. It suggests there might just be one witness to the death who has yet to come forward.'

'Right, I'll do that.'

With *Osprey* locked up, they made their way back down the mooring, Jack directing the PC to *Sunray*, but stopping to chat to the others who had now joined the newly-arrived Hillbecks beside *Whisper*.

'Dexter's been telling us the grim news,' said Lionel. 'Heart attack wasn't it?'

'That's how it seems, but we won't know for sure until after the PM.'

'Rotten timing for me,' complained Harry. 'I'd almost done the deal for

Osprey, but now I'm back to square one.'

'What a shame you've been so inconvenienced,' said Dexter, sarcastically, before turning back to Jack. 'Obviously, that's the rally finished, so what now?'

'First, is to get *Osprey* through the bridge to the yard on the other side and away from public gaze. I'm off to sort a tug, but we'll need some of you to lend a hand.'

'If it means going on that boat, you can count me out,' stated Harry. 'Stiffs give me the creeps, so I'm off.'

'Not as much as the creeps *he* gives me,' said Dexter as Bryant scuttled away.

'But you can count on the rest of us,' assured Lionel, 'except we'll need to lower the mast and funnel first.'

'You can sort that for us, can't you Jim?' said Jack to the engineer. 'Jim ...!'

But Jim Rowston seemed preoccupied with other thoughts as he kept casting nervous glances towards the police car parked nearby. Suddenly realising he was being spoken to, he pulled himself together. 'What? Oh yes ... of course.'

Leaving everyone usefully engaged, Jack made his way up onto the road, only to find Laura crossing the bridge.

'Oh, hello, Jack. I've given my statement to the policeman.' She tapped the overnight bag slung from her shoulder. 'I know it looks bad, my jumping ship like this, but I really do need to get away from here. Mum's got Charles to look after her, so I've called my friend and begged another night's stay until everything's sorted.'

'Probably best. I assumed you wouldn't want to be on *Osprey* tonight anyway.' Jack explained the plan. 'I still think there should be someone keeping an eye on her though. Are you happy for Jim to stay on board while you're in Norwich?'

'Yes, of course, but can you let Mum and Charles know? They're going to stay around to register the death and sort out all the other details. That'll all probably take a few days, so they'll take advantage of the time to do a bit of cruising.'

'I don't blame them, just as long as we can still contact all of you.' Jack glanced along to *Sunbeam*. 'How *is* your mum?'

'Not exactly prostrate with grief if the truth be told,' admitted Laura with a wistful smile. 'Of course, she would never have wished Father dead, but this turn of events has certainly smoothed the way ahead for her and Charles.'

And for several others, thought Jack, as he wished her goodbye and crossed the road into the yard where he pulled out his mobile and rang a familiar listed number.

'Bailey ... Jack Fellows here. Any chance of meeting for a drink and a chat tonight?'

*　　*　　*

'Been a long time, Jack.' On this Monday evening in their favourite pub close by Norwich Cathedral, Detective Inspector Bailey of the Norfolk Constabulary greeted his long-time associate with genuine warmth. 'What is it ... two years?'

'Must be ... that strange business down on the Southern Rivers. Anyway, good to see you, Bailey. Go and find a seat and I'll get your usual.'

Drinks in hand, Jack joined the detective at the quiet corner table. 'So, how's the crime-scene in Norwich these days?'

'Just about under control.' Bailey raised his glass and eyebrows at the same time. 'Cheers, Jack, but tell me about your rivers?'

'As serene and peaceful as ever, Bailey ... or they were until this morning.'

'Why, what happened?'

Jack explained the rally and its tragic ending.

'Bad luck on you, Jack.'

'Even more bad luck on him.' Jack took a sip of his drink. 'Have CID got any details?'

'None, presumably because ...' the DI paused to hold his hands in mock prayer, '... it's not regarded as a suspicious death.'

'Not yet, anyway.'

'"Yet!"' Bailey's glass froze, halfway to his mouth. 'I don't like the sound of that, Jack.'

'Neither do I, seeing as I was supposed to ease them through a stress-free weekend.'

'Seems like the deceased was on dodgy ground, health-wise anyway,' said Bailey after Jack had given him the basic facts, 'but tell me about the others, seeing as that old copper's instinct of yours is obviously troubling you again.'

'Okay.' Jack gave a complete rundown of personalities, and by the time he'd finished, both men's glasses were empty.

Bailey went off for the next round, came back and took a long swig. 'Right, Jack, let me make sure I've got this right. The deceased, this Ralph Lampeter, and his wife, Helen, were estranged because she's now living with a lawyer called Charles Seager, who used to be employed by the deceased, but then got sacked. Wife Helen's been desperate for a divorce so she can marry Seager, but got nowhere due to husband Ralph holding out for a big slice of her inheritance in settlement. At the same time the dead man had been involved, both business-wise and personally, with the wife of another rally member called Dexter Berrington, who also wanted to buy the deceased's boat, but got gazumped.'

'Correct.'

'Blimey!' Bailey sat back and shook his head. 'There's a hornet's nest of relationships if there ever was one. And you say the engineer on his boat *and* the chap who makes parts for it, both have previous?'

'That's right. They were both helped by *New Start*, the charity Ralph Lampeter ran for ex-offenders.' Jack gave the DI a wary look. 'I know what you're thinking, Bailey ... that suspicion must always fall on people with a record.'

'What I'm *actually* thinking,' countered the DI, 'is that none of this is really any business of mine. From what you tell me, no crime's been committed. You say your medic reckoned he died from a cardiac arrest, there were no signs of assault and he had a long-standing heart condition for which he was taking medication.'

'Yes, but not one prescribed by a doctor. I looked up *digitalis* before I came out. It's the old foxglove remedy for *dropsy* that used to be used for heart conditions, but fell out of favour because it needed such precise dosage. Even a small amount extra could be fatal.'

'Which might be what happened with your Mr Lampeter,' concluded Bailey. 'It's not against the law, Jack, to prefer alternative medication, and if your chap accidently overdosed, that's sad, but certainly not warranting a criminal investigation.'

'Perhaps not, but how about the evidence that someone else had been at the death-scene.'

'What the empty wine-glass you told me about?' The DI shrugged. 'That could have been there hours before Lampeter died. Surely members of *Steambuffs* socialise on each other's boats all the time, don't they? Isn't that why they choose to come on a rally together?'

'Yes, but not at midnight, Bailey. And we have the doctor's evidence of Margo Berrington fleeing the scene at just that time.'

'So he says, Jack, but he didn't *see* her, did he? Only the back end of some car he didn't even get the number of.'

'It's not just her though, Bailey. Almost everyone on that rally had some grievance against the deceased.'

Bailey sighed. 'Jack, you know as well as I do that in any group at least one member gets everyone's back up, and I'm sure steam enthusiasts are no different.'

'But, in Ralph Lampeter's case, there are personal reasons for people to actually *hate* him. Even his daughter, Laura, didn't show much affection.'

'Isn't she the *Steambuffs'* secretary who got you into this mess in the first place?' Bailey gave a little chuckle. 'She's the only one you haven't put the finger on, Jack, but she could have a bigger motive than any of them.'

'Such as?'

'That she might stand to inherit some of her old man's money.'

'I don't think there's much to inherit, Bailey. Laura reckoned her father was on hard times, which was why he was selling *Osprey*.'

'Which, presumably, his estranged wife will regain ownership of once more. That's life, Jack ... every death produces winners and losers and lots of accusations ...' Bailey finished his drink and leaned a little closer, '... but, having said that, I've always valued your instincts, mate, so keep me informed and let me know if I can help on the QT at least.'

'Thanks, Bailey, I really appreciate that.' Jack took the DI's glass. 'That's certainly earned you another drink and ...' he hesitated for just a second, '... you'll probably need it when I tell you the other big favour I'm going to ask.'

'Oh no,' groaned the DI, 'here we go!'

*   *   *

Chapter Eight

'Oh no,' groaned Audrey, 'here we go!'

'Crikey, not you too.' It was next morning in the Fellows' household and Jack had just breezed into the kitchen, quite pleased with the telephone calls just made. 'You're sounding just like Bailey.'

'And is it any wonder,' said Audrey, placing her husband's large breakfast cup of coffee on the table with more than a little firmness. 'I know only too well why you're so chirpy, Jack Fellows. You've got your teeth into another investigation, haven't you ... except, this time, I can't see there's any crime to investigate. Even Doctor Edwards told you it was simply a case of death from natural causes.'

'I know that's how it looks on the surface, Aud,' said Jack, sitting down and savouring his first coffee of the day, 'but there were plenty there who wanted Ralph Lampeter dead and now he is. That's too convenient for my liking.'

'More like too straight forward for your liking.' Audrey made an effort to moderate her tone. 'I, more than anyone, know how much you love a good mystery, Jack, but could it be that this time you're letting your imagination run away with you? Why not just relax and let things take their natural course. You've already been on the phone for half an hour this morning. Who was that to?'

'Laura for starters. I've arranged for us to meet her again in Norwich later this morning.'

Audrey put some bread in the toaster and joined her husband at the table. 'You could have checked with me first, Jack,' she chided, slightly annoyed that he was so focussed on pursuing his hunches, that she was being taken for granted. Then the toast popped up, and by the time she sat down again, she'd relented. 'But you're right, love. Laura must be in need of support and it's only proper we try and cheer her up a bit ... but don't go planting seeds of doubt in that poor girl's mind. She's got enough to cope with ... and you said "for starters", so who else were you calling?'

'Dexter Berrington. I've arranged to see him at *ArtVu* in the afternoon, so perhaps a good time for you to get in a bit of shopping, Aud.'

'Meaning you don't want me around for *that* meeting.' Audrey pushed forward the butter and marmalade. 'Well, don't worry, because the last thing I want is to meet Margo again.'

'Not much chance of that,' said Jack with a knowing grin, while liberally buttering his slice of toast.

'How can you be so sure?'

'Oh, I have my ways.'

'Don't I know it,' said Audrey with a sigh. 'All right, Jack, but when we've finished breakfast you'd better take Spike out while I clear up.'

Hearing his name, the collie looked up. Sensing a bit of pre-breakfast tension, he'd kept a low profile so far. Now, mention of the magic word had him up and excited.

'Right.' Jack wolfed down his toast. A walk by the river with Spike would be a good way of mentally taking stock of some of the conflicting issues already clogging his brain.

And also give him time to consider dear Audrey's slant on this whole business. Perhaps she was right and he really was seeing evil intent when there was really only the ways of life ... and death.

*   *   *

Norwich was sunny and bright and not the place for such doubts as, later that morning, he and Audrey made their way to the riverside café where he'd arranged to meet Laura. She was already sitting at one of the outside tables as they strolled up.

'Good to see you both. I hope you don't mind *el fresco*, but I rather feel the need for fresh air and open skies right now.'

'That's understandable.' Jack pulled up chairs and they sat down. 'You had a terrible shock yesterday. How are you feeling now?'

She shrugged and smiled. 'Not too bad. A few nightmares last night and waking up this morning wondering if I'd dreamt the whole thing. But horrors have to be faced and keeping busy seems the best way to do it, so,' she tapped the notebook lying on the table beside her, 'time for more research on my *Telegraph* disaster article.'

Jack looked out across the pedestrian pathway between them and the River Wensum. A hire cruiser was making its way eastward on yet another ebb tide, the dappled water glistening in the morning sun. 'It must have been about here that the explosion took place.'

'Yes, I think it was.' Laura seemed to be deeply affected by a scene she had never witnessed, but probably imagined many times. 'So long ago now, but you can still sense the ghosts of all those poor people and their suffering.'

'So, you do believe in ghosts then, Laura?'

She frowned. 'I'm not sure what I believe, actually, but that's a funny question, Jack. Why do you ask?'

'Only because, less than a week ago, when you had that strange experience at the Great Hospital, you told me you'd seen one.'

'Oh that.' She gave a little embarrassed laugh. 'No, that was just an expression, Jack. I was simply caught up in the atmosphere of the disaster, and letting my imagination run away with me.'

'Okay, but a few days later Charles Seager had a similar experience at the museum, so what did he see?'

'Probably nothing.' She leaned forward confidentially. 'As you know, he was legal officer of RLC, my father's business, and took it pretty hard when it went bust. In fact, he was on the verge of having a full-blown nervous breakdown at the time and, I suspect, still suffers from hallucinations.'

'When was that, Laura?'

'Oh, way back, while I was still at UEA. Mum helped him through it and he kept on working for father for quite a time afterwards until ...'

'... he started the affair with your mum?'

'That's right. After what happened with Margo, Mum was in need of a shoulder to cry on and he was there for her.'

'You mean there was something between your father and Margo *before* your parents split?'

'Yes, a horrible business.'

'Which is why you're so bitter towards her?'

'That obvious is it?' The waitress arrived with the cappuccinos, so it was a minute before Laura could continue, seemingly relieved to be getting something off her chest. 'Well, yes, I really do hate her but, in a way, I blame myself for what happened.' She paused reflectively before continuing. 'I was going home from university for a long weekend break and Margo seemed at a loose end, so I suggested she might like to join me. She was always fun to be with and I thought, with all the tension of the business going under, she'd be just the person to liven things up. But, unfortunately, ...' Laura raised her eyes skyward, '... she was a bit *too* lively for my father to resist.'

'Oh dear,' said Audrey, 'you don't mean they ...?'

'They certainly did, Audrey. The second morning she was there, I took her a cup of tea in bed to get her going and found she already was ... with Father.'

'Goodness! And did your mother find out?'

'Oh yes, inevitably. My parents' marriage had been a bit rocky for a while anyway, but that was the final straw for Mum. From then on they shared the same house but not the same bedroom ... and all thanks to Margo ...' Laura's fingers tightened slightly around her cup, '... the bitch.'

'So, was this when your mum and Charles became ... involved?' probed Audrey.

'Only secretly for a year or so, as Charles was still working as Father's legal advisor, first sorting out the bankruptcy and then later, getting *New Start* established as a regular charity. But as time went on, Mum and Charles became less discreet and Father soon rumbled them.'

'And ...?'

'He went ballistic and gave Charles his marching orders there and then.'

'Hmm. Strange, in that case, that I found the two of them chatting after dinner on Saturday,' said Jack.

'Really?' Laura seemed genuinely surprised. 'Perhaps they were trying to sort some sort of divorce settlement. I know Mum's been wanting Charles to talk to him about it.'

'I gathered it was more about his ghostly fright at the museum. He seemed to think your father would be equally shocked by it.'

'I can't think why,' said Laura, finishing her cappuccino. 'Anyway, without sounding callous, what's happened at least makes life simpler for Mum now.'

'Have you spoken to her since yesterday?'

'Oh yes, I rang her later last night and then first thing this morning. Of course, like me, she's still pretty shocked, but I also detected a sense of relief that she and Charles can now get on with their lives.'

'You mean by finally getting married?'

'That and life generally.'

'And with your mum's inheritance still intact,' added Jack, a little more subjectively. 'Will she be taking over *Osprey* again?'

'Only the boat's ownership. *Osprey's* always been too big for us to operate just for pleasure, and after what happened yesterday, Mum just wants to be shot of her as soon as possible. The way she was talking, I got the impression she's going to offer *Osprey* to Dexter for a nominal sum, knowing he'll look after the boat and make good use of it.'

'Good news for Dexter.'

'Yes, and I can understand how Mum feels. I don't want to go on *Osprey* again either, but I'll probably have to, seeing as there are still some things of Father's on board we need to clear.'

'I might be able to help you there,' offered Jack. 'I'm back patrolling on the river tomorrow and plan to stop by Ludham Bridge. If you want, I could collect your father's kit off the boat and, at the same time, check how Jim Rowston's making out.'

'Oh, that would be great. Thank you. And give Jim my best wishes when you see him. I expect he's wondering where all this will leave him.'

'Perhaps better off than he was expecting. If Dexter can get *Osprey* for a reasonable amount and his trip-boat business takes off, he might be able to take Jim on as well.'

'A nice thought,' said Laura, 'but if Dexter does make any money, that wife of his will milk him of every penny.'

'You're probably right.' Jack finished his coffee and stood up. 'It's been good talking, Laura, but other places to go, so we'll be off.'

'Yes, I've got lots to do too, but I'll walk with you as far as Foundry Bridge.'

Strolling back up Riverside, with the peace of the river on one side and the roar of road traffic on the other, seemed a good time to put some space between the painful past and the acceptable present. Only as they neared the bridge did Jack choose to raise an even more sensitive issue. 'Don't take this the wrong way, Laura, but if it came to it, would you have any independent witnesses who'd vouch for your movements around midnight on Sunday?'

She looked a little startled. 'You mean an alibi for the time of Father's death? Goodness, why? Is there any reason to think it was anything other than a heart attack?'

'It all depends on the post mortem but, in cases like this, you always have to be prepared for the less-than-obvious.'

'But you think there was something suspicious?'

'There are certainly puzzling aspects which the police might follow up. Best to be prepared, just in case.'

'Right.' She gulped slightly. 'Well, that night we went for a late supper at an Indian restaurant on Prince of Wales Road. I should think they'll remember us there. After that we went straight back to the flat, but happened to run into the neighbours just back from the cinema. We invited them in and ended up chatting until the early hours.'

'Sounds like you're pretty well covered then,' assured Jack as they prepared to go their separate ways. 'I'll give you a call when I've got your father's stuff and then I can update you on what's happening. In the meantime, keep your chin up and let me know any other way I can help.'

'Thanks, Jack, for that and everything else.'

'Why didn't you tell her you were off to see Dexter this afternoon?' asked Audrey as Laura continued along Riverside and she and Jack turned up Prince of Wales Road.

'Better for all concerned if she doesn't know,' was all Jack would admit to as they set off into the city.

*   *   *

ArtVu lay nestled in a narrow side-street just off the bustling thoroughfare of Gentlemen's Walk, its one large window now displaying a framed print of Cromer Beach. Though it filled the window, Jack could still see how a figure peering in would have been instantly recognised by Margo standing inside. Today, entering to the accompaniment of the jangling doorbell, he was glad to see it was only Dexter behind the counter.

'Good to see you, Jack.' The ex-mariner smiled and glanced about the empty gallery. 'Just squeeze your way through all the customers.'

'Yes, not exactly crowding in are they?' Which was a shame, thought Jack because, being in such a prime location, it could have been a goldmine with more imaginative merchandise for sale. He looked around. 'I don't see Margo's artwork on display anywhere, Dexter.'

'That's because she's given up producing any. It's a pity, because she was really talented, but by the time I met her she seemed to have lost interest in painting *and* running *ArtVu* ...' he gave a heavy sigh, '... so here I am, as usual, left to the day-to-day running of her gallery, sitting in an empty shop and staring at the walls. Not the best of lives for someone who loved life at sea and a bit of action.'

'But at least one that's given you time to dream up a trip-boat business. I presume that could now be on the cards again?'

Dexter visibly brightened. 'Yes. Helen gave me a call this morning and said she'd like to discuss the prospect of selling *Osprey* to me after all.'

'One in the eye for Bryant then?'

'Yes, thank God. I let him skipper *Pickle* back to Stalham yesterday after all the fuss had died down and, believe me, the man's a menace when it comes to boat-handling. He bashed into several boats and, of course, always blamed the other skipper and shouted a load of abuse to add insult to injury. I spent the whole trip apologising on his behalf. Poor *Pickle*'s reputation was shattered in the space of an hour.' Dexter closed his eyes briefly. 'I tell you, Jack, it was hard enough handing my pride-and-joy over to him, but knowing she would probably end up as a wreck was truly heartbreaking.'

'He'd do even more damage with a big boat like *Osprey*,' pointed out Jack. 'Let's hope that won't happen now.'

'It won't if I can help it, but don't forget I still have Margo's problem to

89

sort. It's all very well being offered *Osprey* at a reduced price, but an empty prospect if I still don't have the cash. Bryant was supposed to pay me for *Pickle* yesterday, but said he's waiting for clearance from the bank or some such excuse.'

'Keep at him then and make sure you get it, Dexter,' warned Jack. 'I never did trust that man and if he realises you can't buy *Osprey* until he pays up, he'll hold out until it's too late for you. Meantime, let's try and sort out Margo's problem.'

'I don't see how.' Dexter shrugged broad shoulders. 'She refuses to tell me why she's being threatened or by whom. It would have been good if you could have talked to her this afternoon, but the police called her into the station to chat about Lampeter's death. Apparently there are some issues that need clarifying, though goodness knows how Margo can help.'

'Standard procedure, Dexter, but she should also tell them she's being blackmailed while she has the opportunity.'

'Not much chance of that, I'm afraid. She reckons it's more than her life's worth.'

'Okay, well let's see if we can suss it out for ourselves.' Jack nodded towards the display window. 'That's where she saw the mysterious figure gazing at her painting?'

'That's right, at a water colour she'd painted long before I met her. I can't see how *it* can be connected, but after that scare she told me to trash it.' Dexter looked a little guilty. 'I suppose I should have done as she asked, but it seemed too good to just destroy, so I managed to hide it upstairs instead. Want to see it?'

'Yes please.'

Dexter was soon back with a large framed painting. 'Here it is. I've studied it a dozen times since that weird day and still can't see anything sinister in the damn thing.'

'Wow, it's a stunning painting.' Jack studied the work depicting a wooded landscape set amongst slightly undulating terrain and with a glittering sea sparkling in the distance. 'You say Margo painted it soon after she left art college?'

'That's right. She'd got a good degree and, as you can see, she was a gifted artist.'

'Absolutely, so I wonder why she didn't sell it then?'

'I really don't know. She always made excuses and insisted that she wasn't happy with it, so it just hung in our flat all those years.'

'Until it was displayed in the window just a week or so ago. Why the sudden change?'

'That was my doing, Jack. Like I said, Margo hadn't produced anything in years and we needed to sell something, so I suggested we give this one a try.'

'And she agreed?'

'Reluctantly ... yes.'

Jack lifted the painting onto the counter and studied it in greater detail. 'This looks to me very much like the North Norfolk Coast.'

Dexter nodded. 'It could well be. I know Margo used to paint up there a lot.'

'But she didn't tell you the exact location?'

'No. Said she'd lost interest in painting and needed to put all her spare time and energy into setting up *ArtVu*.'

'Which she's now also lost interest in.' Jack glanced around the gallery with its mediocre stock and air of neglect. 'So why does she keep the business going?'

'That's what I keep asking her, but she won't hear of off-loading it.'

'Even though it loses money?'

'Yes.'

'When did she first buy it?'

'About a year before we met.'

Jack stood back and folded his arms. 'You see, Dexter, what puzzles me is how a young artist, fresh out of art school, found the kind of money to set up a gallery like this in the first place?'

'I know, but she said it was thanks to being left a sizeable inheritance, including some very valuable antiques which she sold. The way I understand it, having bought *ArtVu* with the money, she soon realised that antique dealing was far more profitable than art and decided to pursue that line instead.'

'An enterprising girl then, but interesting that she bought the gallery not long after doing a painting she never sold.' He nodded towards the mystery landscape. 'Mind if I photograph it?'

'Help yourself, though I can't see it will help much.'

'I still think it might shed some light on what's happening. Blackmail's a very serious crime, Dexter, and Margo needs to tread very carefully, especially in the light of what happened on Sunday.'

'Lampeter's death?' Dexter straightened up in surprise. 'You think there might be something more to that than meets the eye.'

'There might be.'

'But you surely don't suspect that Margo was involved?'

'She was involved *with* him, Dexter, and that would be enough to put her

91

straight at the top of the suspect list if the police get their teeth into it. The more we know before that happens, the better prepared you'll be.'

'Okay, Jack, I trust you to do what's best.'

'I'll try, and start by taking these photos.'

Job done, Jack left Dexter to his empty gallery and headed off for his pre-arranged teatime rendezvous with Audrey, wondering as he went if the ex-mariner would have been quite so helpful if he'd known the real reason for Margo's absence with the police. Jack smiled to himself. Sometimes though, when it came to deviousness, the end justified the means.

*   *   *

'I can't believe you did that, Jack Fellows,' scolded Audrey, pouring their tea in a quiet corner of the café. 'I wouldn't want to be in your shoes if Margo ever finds out you'd asked DI Bailey to call her into the police station just so you could have some time alone with her husband.' Then she allowed herself just a smile of satisfaction. 'Mind you, it probably gave the little madam something to think about.'

'The main thing is though, that I got these,' said Jack, sliding across his mobile phone and the photos he'd taken of Margo's watercolour.

'It's a lovely painting, but I can't see anything special about it,' said Audrey as she studied the images. 'Surely it was just a coincidence that this picture happened to be on display in the window when she spotted her supposed blackmailer.'

'I rather think it was the other way round,' said Jack, helping himself to a cake. 'The way I see it, it was the painting that first got his attention, and *then* Margo Berrington. Think about it. Why else would she want the thing trashed after the incident? So, for the moment, let's concentrate on the painting. Where do you reckon it is?'

'The North Norfolk Coast by the look of it.'

'That's what I thought, so why has Margo always been so secretive about it?'

'Presumably, you aim to find the answer.'

'*We're* going to find the answer, Aud,' corrected Jack.

'Are we now?' Audrey re-scanned the image. 'You're assuming it is an *actual* place, Jack. How do you know it isn't just a made-up scene?'

'I think a bit of it was ... which will be the most significant aspect when we find it.'

'*If* we find it,' cautioned Audrey. 'I can see us wasting an awful lot of time and petrol searching the county for a place that may not even exist.'

'Not if we do it methodically,' said Jack, pocketing the phone, 'starting this evening, so drink up, Aud, and let's get going.'

'Oh Jack,' muttered Audrey resignedly under her breath, as her dearly-loved husband went to pay their bill. She was thinking of all the days of investigation that lay ahead – puzzling over evidence, analysing facts, discussing suspicions, offering theories. Jack would love it and she would just go along with it as she always did.

Except this time it all seemed somewhat pointless. Pursuing a suspicion regarding Ralph Lampeter's death would surely lead nowhere. Margo Berrington had probably got herself in a fix, but it was nothing more than she deserved and this whole painting thing was obviously going to be another complete wild goose chase. Ah well, if it got her a trip to North Norfolk, it wouldn't be all bad.

Seeing Jack all settled up and ready to go, she joined him at the exit. 'We just need to buy ourselves an OS map before we head homeward,' he remembered as they stepped outside. 'Then tonight we can pin down just where Margo painted that landscape of hers.'

*   *   *

'I still think this is going to be like searching for a needle in a haystack, Jack,' said Audrey, rescuing her favourite mug from being swept onto the floor as her husband spread the newly-purchased Ordnance Survey map across the kitchen table.

But, with Spike walked, evening meal eaten and dishwasher loaded, Jack was clearly ready for action. 'Have faith, Aud.' Refolding the map to just its upper half, he laid his mobile, with its photos of Margo's painting, beside it. 'All we need to do is match what's on here to the same place on the map.'

'If it *is* on here.'

But Jack was in no mood for negative thinking. 'Big skies, undulating ground, sea and coast... this *has* to be the area.'

'But a vast one, Jack.' Audrey studied the image of the painting more closely, particularly the elevation from which it had been painted. 'She certainly must have been high up to get this view.'

'You're right, Aud, and that should help us zero into the spot, together with this.' He was pointing to a railway line depicted in the painting's middle distance with the smoke trail of a steam train streaming back through wooded scenery.

Audrey sighed. 'Are you sure it's true to life, Jack? Or do you think she simply used her imagination to create a lovely image of rural nostalgia?'

'I'm absolutely sure it's authentic, Aud, because that steam train's not made up. Just think where one's still operating up there.'

'Of course, the North Norfolk Railway at Sheringham.'

'Exactly, and you can see how the train in the painting has crossed a road, which could be here.'

Audrey followed Jack's finger to a wooded area on the map, interlaced with small trails, just a mile or so inland from the sea. 'But that's at Sheringham Park – one of our favourite National Trust walking places – so, she must have been on a hill to get that uninterrupted view.'

'Not a hill, Aud. Something we've been up ourselves and from where you can see for miles.'

'The Gazebo!' exclaimed Audrey, remembering the high viewing platform that provided a tree top vista of the magnificent parkland and its surrounding countryside with the sea beyond. 'Of course, the perfect place to paint a landscape.'

'And where we need to go to check this out,' said Jack, refolding the map. 'I'm back patrolling on the river again tomorrow, but the day after we'll have ourselves a recce.'

'But what do you expect to find?'

'I'm not sure, but hopefully the place itself will tell us when we get there.'

Audrey wasn't so sure, but before she could discuss it further, the telephone rang.

*   *   *

Racing up the stairs to take the call, Jack tossed the OS map onto his desk and grabbed the phone. 'Bailey, good to hear from you. What's the word?'

'The pathology report on Ralph Lampeter ...' the DI's low voice had the weary tone of someone who'd already dealt with too much paperwork for one day, '... I thought you'd want to hear the preliminary results.'

'You bet. Go ahead.'

'Well, he died from a heart attack all right, about midnight just as thought.'

'How about his *digitalis* content though?'

'Still waiting for a toxicology report on that, Jack, but we have tracked down the herbalist who prescribed it. Apparently the deceased always held a distrust of doctors, but this practitioner turned out to be completely kosher ... a registered herbalist who confirmed he'd prescribed and supplied the substance, but that he'd always warned Lampeter of the dangers of overdosing or mixing it with alcohol.'

'Right, so how about that whisky sample I got the constable to bring you?'

'You were correct in your suspicions there as well, Jack. It contained well over a lethal dose of the stuff.'

'There you are then. Suspicious circumstances, so now you can get on and start an investigation.'

'Yes, but not a criminal one, Jack. It was Lampeter's own medication added to his favourite tipple so, until you show me something to the contrary, we're probably going to treat this as an accidental overdose or suicide.'

'Suicide!' Jack made an effort to lower his own voice. 'Why would Lampeter want to top himself, for crikey's sake?'

'A few reasons, by the sound of it. He had money issues, a broken marriage, a failed business and probably a lot of stress from this charity he was running.'

'You're suddenly well informed, Bailey,' said Jack, suspiciously. 'I'm guessing all that came from this afternoon's meeting with Margo Berrington.'

'It might have,' admitted the DI. 'I didn't interview her myself, but the constable who did, reckoned she was very much on the defensive and quite ready to sow the seeds of doubt about several of this *Steambuffs'* lot.'

'Who she'll be more than happy to stab in the back, Bailey. Don't forget her car was spotted at the scene that night and she *had* fallen out with the deceased. What I really want to know right now, though, is did you give her a cup of tea like I asked?'

'Of course we did, but until I've got more evidence, I'm still treating this death as suicide.' Bailey sighed. 'The man surely had complications in his life, Jack, and a feisty girlfriend and a heart problem on top of it all. Let's face it, if you wanted to top yourself, some of your own medication in a glass of best malt whisky sounds as good a way to go as any.'

'*If* he wanted to, which I don't think he did, Bailey. On the contrary, I think he had more going for him than anyone realised.'

'Care to elaborate?'

'Not until I have more proof, but how about Harry Bryant? Did you find anything on him?'

'Quite a bit, actually, and you were correct in your suspicions there, because he's definitely got form.' Over the phone came the sound of Bailey turning papers. 'Ten years ago he did a stretch for possession.'

'Of what?'

'High quality antiques stolen from a large country house up in North Norfolk.'

'Now, that *is* interesting,' said Jack, straightening up in his chair. 'Anything else?'

'Only that the lads who got him were pretty sure he was the actual thief, but couldn't prove it. In the end, they settled for him just getting three years for handling the stuff.'

'But he managed to set up an engineering business soon after release, which shows he could still lay his hands on money.'

'Doubtless from ill-gotten gains he'd stashed away from previous jobs,' said Bailey. 'The suspicion was that he'd been housebreaking for years before they finally got him for this.'

'So, did they recover all the antiques from this last job?'

There was a pause as Bailey flicked through more pages of the report. 'No, only about half, and the less valuable half at that.'

'So the more valuable items still haven't been recovered. Can you get me an inventory of what they were, Bailey, and the house they were taken from?'

'You don't ask for much, do you? I know I owe you, Jack, but you're fast running out of favours.'

'That's all right because, if I get to the bottom of all this, you'll probably owe me more. But how about the other record I asked you to check?'

'James Rowston, the marine engineer ... seems a case of a good guy going wrong, Jack. His life had been unblemished until he was caught coming ashore from a Far East trip with a load of dope. Seeing as he tested negative for drugs himself, the police suspected he was planning to sell it on the street. He swore it was only for personal use, had a good lawyer, and managed to get two years for "possession" rather than "dealing".'

'Still a stiff term for a first offence, Bailey.'

'I know, but he refused to reveal any details of how or where he got the stuff, so he got the full tariff.'

'Interesting.'

'In what way?'

'Just that he doesn't seem the type to line the pockets of drug dealers, let alone show them any loyalty. Anyway,' concluded Jack, 'I appreciate all the info, Bailey. I'm back on the river tomorrow, so perhaps we can meet later for a drink.'

'If I ever get all the drinks you owe me, Jack, I'll probably get drummed out of the force for alcoholism,' grumbled the DI.

'In which case, you'd do better sticking to tea,' warned Jack, '... talking of which, what I need is your report on that cup of it they gave Margo Berrington yesterday.'

Chapter Nine

A cup of something hot would have been welcomed by Jack the next morning as he backed his patrol launch from its Irstead boathouse and out onto the River Ant. With a nip in the fresh, clear air, it was that moment of the day's awakening he always loved as the river life stirred and he could ponder his own place in its conception.

Inevitably, those thoughts wandered into the darker side of human nature and, as the launch's engine warmed and he checked equipment, Jack considered, yet again, just why he allowed himself to become involved in its devious ways.

In the end, he decided it was simply copper's instinct, coupled with an inbuilt sense of integrity that wrongs had to be righted and moral values upheld. Once again, fate had thrown a jigsaw of suspicious and mysterious pieces that needed to be fitted together to form a picture and he knew he wouldn't rest until it was complete.

For the moment though, he was happy with this immediate one of Irstead, as he turned downriver and once more glided through the tree-lined shoals before merging into more open marshland. It certainly seemed longer than just forty-eight hours since he'd last enjoyed this passage, at the wheel of an old steamboat and with little thought of just how tragic events would ultimately turn.

Something that hadn't changed though was the river itself. One of the narrowest of the Broadland rivers, the Ant was also, in the opinion of many, by far the prettiest. This early morning, like most, there were plenty of boats moored to its banks and showing little sign of life, save for the tempting smell of frying breakfasts. Nearing How Hill, a coil of smoke drifting lazily upwards from a small inlet indicated something different and, as he drew nearer, he was pleased to see it was *Sunbeam*, lying in sheltered seclusion, her mooring lines tied to nearby trees and Helen and Seager enjoying an early coffee up for'ard. As Jack slowed to wave, Helen recognised the launch and beckoned him onboard. Within minutes he was alongside and joining them in the cockpit.

'Don't let me intrude.'

'Not at all. We were up at the crack of dawn and Charles has almost finished his breakfast, haven't you, darling?'

'Almost. Too bloody cold to lie-in.' Charles Seager seemed a little less enthusiastic at the ranger's unexpected company, but already Helen was ushering Jack into one of the cockpit seats and producing a mug.

'Coffee?'

'Please.' Soon Jack was settling back into the well padded upholstery and warming his hands on the steaming mug he'd just been handed. 'So you obviously night-stopped here.'

'Yes.' Helen topped up her own mug from the brass urn that seemed almost an integral part of the boat's boiler, and sat down opposite. 'We felt the need to escape all the trauma of Sunday and head back upriver to Sutton Staithe and another night of comfort. But we stopped at How Hill for a walk, left it a bit late and, as it was such a lovely evening, decided to stop here instead for a night on board.'

'I don't blame you.' Hanging over this cut were the drooping branches of a willow that would provide welcome shade to the grassy banks as the sun rose higher. 'You need a peaceful spot like this to come to terms with all that's happened.'

'I think we already have, Jack. To be honest, neither of us is harbouring much grief for my estranged husband.' She gave a guilty smile. 'Does that sound awful?'

'No. I can quite understand it after all you've put up with.'

She looked questioningly over the rim of her coffee mug. 'So you know the story of Charles and me?'

'Yes, Laura told me.'

Helen nodded sadly. 'It must have been a rotten time for her. The family business had gone bust and she inevitably felt some responsibility for bringing Margo into our home and scuppering the marriage. After that I found comfort with Charles, and Ralph was completely wrapped up in his *New Start* charity. And then poor Laura had her own heart broken.'

'Yes, she hinted at busting up with a boyfriend, though she didn't go into detail.'

'Why should she?' said Seager, pushing his plate to one side. 'It was no big deal.'

'It was for her, Charles,' protested Helen. 'Laura was convinced he was *the* one and hasn't dated anyone since. The poor girl went through a terrible time.'

'Yes, well, I'm sure Fellows won't want boring with all the details.'

'Actually, I would,' replied Jack, knowing it was now or never time to fill in some gaps, '... if you don't mind sharing it with me.'

'Not at all. I'm sure Laura won't mind me telling you, and Ralph can't object as he's no longer with us anyway.' Helen put her cup down. 'It happened after she'd graduated and was establishing herself as a freelance journalist. Ralph had set up the *New Start* charity with the help of Charles and, as our home was its registered office, he needed more space and got a young builder called Peter Warmstead to do the work. Peter was good at his job and attractive in a rugged sort of way. When he and Laura set eyes on each other, I think it was love at first sight. I accepted it as just a summer romance, but Ralph was against it from the start.'

'With good reason,' butted in Seager. 'He thought Warmstead just wasn't good enough for his daughter.'

'Were you still working for Ralph at this time?' Jack asked.

'Yes, as legal officer for the charity.'

'And *you* had dealings with this young man?'

'Not particularly ... at least not until he went and took something that wasn't his.'

Jack's eyebrows rose, but it was Helen who explained. 'Ralph found a lot of money missing from his desk drawer.'

'And it had to be Warmstead who'd stolen it,' added Seager. 'He was the only person with access to the office. When the police arrived, they found it stashed in his van.'

'You called the police?'

'Of course. How else do you deal with theft?'

'It depends.' Jack turned back to Helen. 'So, was this Peter Warmstead one of the ex-offenders your husband used to employ?'

'Good Lord, no. He was just a local lad with good references.'

'But you pressed charges?'

'We did indeed,' answered Seager, 'but, in the event, it never came to trial because Warmstead simply skipped the country.'

'To India, of all places,' added Helen, 'where he got a job working for an overseas aid organisation building schools in remote areas.'

'He can't have been all bad then, but how did Laura take it?'

'She was devastated, as you can imagine. She just couldn't believe Peter would do such a thing. It was so out of character and she felt very betrayed and let down. I'm sure that's why she hasn't been interested in going out with anyone else. She just doesn't want to risk being hurt again.'

'And did she ever hear any more from Warmstead?'

'No, the next thing she knew of him was a year or so later when his death was reported in the newspapers.'

'Death!'

'Yes, he and a workmate were in Jaipur and got caught up in some terrorist bombings. Peter was one of the many killed.'

'The "Pink City bombings",' recalled Jack. 'Nine bomb blasts in fifteen minutes that killed eighty and injured a hundred and seventy. I remember reading the report at The Yard.'

It was Seager's turn to raise his eyebrows. '*Scotland* Yard?'

'That's right. Didn't I tell you? I was a CID officer for many years before retirement.'

'I see,' said Seager, noticeably moderating his tone.

'But now I have this job ... which I need to get back to,' said Jack, finishing his coffee. 'My next stop'll be Ludham Bridge to check on *Osprey*.'

'Yes, Laura told me on the phone last night that you'd kindly agreed to collect Ralph's things,' said Helen. 'She also told me you weren't convinced his death was natural.'

'No, and I'm still not, Helen. There are certain inconsistencies that the police may need to have explained.'

'Police!' exclaimed Seager, sitting up.

'Yes. You, of all people, should know they always get involved when a death is suspicious.'

'Why? Do they think it was suicide?'

'Or worse,' said Jack, studying the lawyer's reaction. 'Anyway, it's important that *Osprey* stays secure for the moment, which is why it's good for you to have Jim Rowston keeping an eye on her.'

'Poachers always make the best gamekeepers,' muttered Seager, cynically, 'but probably just as well for security reasons. No doubt there are things on board worth stealing.'

'People about here are pretty honest,' said Jack, 'but there was one item already missing from the boat that you might know about.'

Helen frowned. 'Why, what's gone?'

'A rather handsome Georgian coffee pot that I'd admired when I first went on the boat. After your husband's death I noticed it was missing.'

'Oh, that thing.' Helen gave a dismissive snort. 'Ralph bought it for the boat soon after we split, mainly, I think, because it had *Osprey*'s initial engraved on it.'

'Do you have any idea where he bought it?'

Helen scratched her head for just a few seconds. 'Yes, come to think of it, he bought it off Margo.'

'Margo Berrington?'

'Yes, but she wasn't married then. She and Laura had just ended their friendship and Margo was trying to bolster her sale of paintings with a bit of antique-dealing. That pot's certainly not something I would want,' concluded Helen, dismissively.

'If it was worth something, it was doubtless nicked by that scoundrel Bryant,' suggested Seager. 'He probably thought no-one would notice. That man's trouble and I wouldn't trust him an inch.'

'That's one thing we do both agree on,' said Jack, handing back his mug. 'Anyway, time I was off. Thanks for the coffee.'

'Not at all,' said Helen, joining him at the gunwale as he climbed back into his launch. 'And please keep me informed, Jack. Ralph and I might have gone our separate ways, but I still want to know how he died and why.'

'So do I. In the meantime, try and enjoy the rest of your cruising, and I'm sure I'll see you again soon.'

But perhaps not under such pleasant circumstances, thought Jack as he got under way again and *Sunbeam* drew astern. That chance meeting and chat had been worthwhile even if, like so many others in the last few days, it had raised almost as many new questions as answers.

He continued down the Ant. Perhaps Jim Rowston might shed a bit more light on this whole strange business.

* * *

Forty-five minutes and Ludham Bridge was in sight, busy as usual with boats moored both sides of the river. Why then did he have that old feeling of unease, as though events were once more conspiring against this popular mooring place? With increasing foreboding, he continued on under the bridge and, as he did so, a police car went wailing overhead before turning right, straight into the boatyard.

Something had obviously happened and Jack's first instinct was to check for *Osprey*. The old steamboat was still there, but the yard itself was alive with uniforms and emergency vehicles. Alongside, he collared one of the yardhands. 'What's going on? What's up?'

The worker nodded back in the direction of *Osprey*. 'That chap you left on the boat ...'

'Jim Rowston ... what about him?'

'He's dead.'

* * *

Years of police service had made Jack reasonably immune to shocking events, but he was still trying to come to terms with this one, when a familiar voice called him from alongside *Osprey*.

'Jack ... over here.'

'Bailey ... am I glad to see you. What on earth's happened?'

'Another death, Jack ... the boat's engineer by the look of it.' The DI paused to give some brief instructions to a young female DC before turning back to Jack. 'One of the chaps from the boatyard called by early this morning to talk to him about shifting the steamer to a different mooring. Not getting any response, he went on board and found him dead in his bunk. Our doctor's just confirmed the cause was heart related, sometime around midnight.'

'Just like Ralph Lampeter.'

'Looks that way, which is why you've got me here this time. A second death like this in two days is stretching things even for me.'

'Me too.' Jack turned and faced *Osprey*, with its memories of a man who'd already had more than his share of life's angst. 'Is his body still onboard?'

Bailey shook his head. 'No, the coroner's men took it an hour ago after CSI had done their initial examinations. They're just wrapping up now.'

As if on cue, a team in hooded white coveralls filed off *Osprey*. 'That's us done, sir.'

'Good. Anything you can tell me at this stage?'

'Not much, but we lifted two sets of prints, one belonging to the deceased.'

'Any ID on the other?'

'Not yet, other than we found them all over the boat.'

'So, probably belonging to one of your rally members, Jack.'

'Possibly.' Jack turned to the senior CSI man. 'Was there any evidence the deceased had been drinking whisky before his death?'

'Not that we could see.'

'Hmm.'

'You're obviously thinking on the same lines as me, Jack,' said Bailey as the CSI team went on their way. 'That he'd been helping himself to the boat's tipple to while away the lonesome hours?'

'It was a thought.'

'Yeah, but I've checked, and all the bottles were taken off for testing after the first death.'

'Which rules out that possibility then?'

'Looks like it ...' Bailey turned back to *Osprey*, '... but you time for a quick chat?'

'Of course.'

Back in *Osprey*'s saloon, the DI stood for a minute admiring the boat's wood-panelled opulence. 'So, this is how the other half live ...' he plonked down onto one of the built-in couches, '... except the last two blokes on here didn't did they, Jack, so what do you reckon?'

'Too soon to speculate, Bailey. I'm still trying to grasp what's actually happened. I only came today to collect Lampeter's stuff for the family and check Jim was okay.'

'Which he certainly wasn't.' The DI leaned forward. 'So, do you want to hear my theories?'

'Go ahead.'

'I've got a couple, actually. One, that Rowston really was a former drug user and, left alone on the boat, went back to his old ways and perhaps took some contaminated dope.'

'That certainly doesn't fit with the character I knew, but the autopsy will show whether you're right,' said Jack 'What's your other theory?'

'That he had some hand in Lampeter's death and, feeling remorse and realising he no longer had a job, took an overdose of *digitalis* himself.'

'But that medication was taken off the boat for examination.'

'Perhaps he knew of another bottle stashed away somewhere.'

'Unlikely and, again, completely out of character, Bailey. Jim Rowston was one man I would have really trusted, and what possible motive could he have anyway?'

Bailey shrugged. 'A bad fall out ... caught doing something he shouldn't ... or perhaps some event from the past had reared its ugly head.'

'Except Jim couldn't have murdered Lampeter, because he was in Yarmouth the night it happened.'

'That's what he said, but do you know for sure, Jack? Perhaps that's where he'd arranged to meet a dealer, bought himself an eightball of hard stuff, came back early, got discovered by the boss and ended up killing him.' The DI shrugged. 'Anyway, too late to ask him, but we could certainly check his movements if we decided to investigate further.'

'I think it's time to start checking what *everyone* was doing that night, Bailey. In the meantime, I'm thinking of Jim Rowston as a victim rather than a suspect.' Jack looked around at the old boat's interior, so recently the only home the engineer had known. 'Have you made contact with any of his family yet?'

'No, and I was hoping you might help there by letting Laura Lampeter know what's happened and finding out from her his next-of-kin.'

'I'll try,' promised Jack. 'It's the least I can do in exchange for the details you're about to give me.'

The DI took the hint. 'Ah, yes, the North Norfolk manor house robbery. It turns out the house was owned by the Otterton family, but chummy pretty well cleaned them out of family gold, silver and heirlooms.' Bailey pulled a folded sheet from his inside pocket and handed it across. 'Here's the printout of the items never recovered.'

Jack quickly scanned the long list of valuables. 'Crikey, this reads like an auction catalogue at Sotheby's.' With his finger going down the items, he finally alighted on one. 'Ah, this is what I was looking for.'

'Glad it's helped,' muttered Bailey with mock sarcasm. 'Are you going to let me in on the secret?'

'I might after tomorrow. Audrey and I are taking a little trip up to the north coast to test another theory I have.'

The DI sighed. 'Yeah, well don't keep me in the dark too long will you. With this second death following so soon after the first, the Chief Constable's going to be demanding results, and fast.'

'Which means you've shelved the suicide theory then?'

'What do you think, with a second death on the same boat within forty-eight hours? No, this looks like at least one case of murder, Jack and any leads you've got will be much appreciated.'

'And I'll be glad to share them with you, Bailey. Jim Rowston was a good man and I want to see whoever was responsible for his death brought to justice. But I'm going to need information which you'll get easier than me. How about that cup of tea you gave Margo. What were those results?'

'As you probably suspected, Jack. Her prints on the cup were the same as those on the wine glass found next to the body. What do you reckon? Lover's tiff?'

'If so, it can't be connected to Jim's death. But I'm already thinking in wider circles than mere personal relationships. What I need is for you to check something further afield.'

'How much further?'

'Here.' Jack quickly scribbled some notes into his own pocketbook, tore out the page and handed it across.'

Bailey's eyes widened. 'Why do you want me to contact them?'

'Because they'll, hopefully, provide the answers to most of the strange happenings this last weekend.'

*   *   *

'Oh, poor Jim. You always said what a good man he was.' It was late evening in the Fellows' household, Audrey clearing the dishes, darkness outside and a sombre mood within after she'd just finished listening to Jack's account of the day's sad event.

'Yes, in spite of some of the mistakes he might have made in life, I always thought him a man of integrity.' Jack threw his napkin onto the table and sat back in his chair. 'Sadly, I never did get to hear his full story, but I'm guessing it was a bit less shadowy than some of the other characters on this rally.'

'You mean like Bryant?'

'And others,' said Jack, scornfully. 'Jim certainly had some skeletons in his closet, but I'm thinking they were due to circumstances rather than his making.'

'But you think his death was suspicious and perhaps linked to Ralph Lampeter's?'

'Yes, but not for reasons that might be apparent. My hunch is that Jim died as a *result* of Ralph's death and not *because* of it.'

'Yes, well, you can explain that properly when you know all the facts,' said Audrey. 'But you do seem to have had an interesting early morning chat with Helen and Charles.'

'*Very* interesting, and we were right in thinking Laura had suffered a broken heart when she was younger.'

'Did you get the details?'

'No, and right now I'm more concerned with another inconsistency our chat brought up.'

'Which was?'

'That Margo had started selling antiques just *before* she received the inheritance Dexter assumed she used to buy the gallery and set up *ArtVu*.'

'Is that particularly significant?'

'It is when I combine it with the one other small mystery connected to *Osprey*. Having said that, I'm pretty certain Helen told me the truth and that neither she nor Charles know anything about this strange business of Margo and the painting.'

'... but which tomorrow's investigation might solve ...' Audrey put a hand on Jack's, '... unless that visit's off after today's sad event.'

'No, we'll still go, Aud. More than ever I want to get this sorted and, anyway, a change of scene will do us both good.'

Audrey nodded agreement. 'You're probably right, and Spike will certainly enjoy a run in the woods.'

Hearing mention of his name and walks would normally have had the collie by the door with tail wagging. He was certainly reacting now, but in a disturbed way, up and alert with ears pricked and giving a low growl that quickly turned into a warning bark.

Jack knew those reactions. 'He's heard something, Aud.' From the garden came the sound of a breaking twig underfoot. 'There's someone out there. Wait here.' Heading to the utility room and grabbing his torch, he was about to ease open the back door when a piercing scream from Audrey had him tearing back. He dashed in to find her staring fixatedly out of the window, hands clutched to her throat and visibly shaking. 'Good Lord, love, what is it?'

Audrey managed to take one hand away enough to point a quivering finger out into the garden. 'Jack ... out there ... I've just seen a ghost.'

*   *   *

Now was not the time for questions or details, but to nail this mystery once and for all. Seeing a figure already backing away from the window, Jack raced out, Spike at his side and oblivious to Audrey's call to "be careful".

Already the figure, whether real or ethereal, was fast disappearing towards the shrubbery and had almost reached the far garden wall by the time first Spike, and then Jack, caught up. Faced with a barking dog and a burly man, the intruder turned to face them, but Jack's momentum was in no mood for compromise as it carried him headlong into what was a far-from-spiritual form. Locked now in violent embrace, the two crashed down together into Audrey's prized rhododendrons.

'Right, mate, you're nicked,' gasped Jack, the old vernacular returning quicker than his breath as he pulled back the black hood to reveal a face both sad and defiant.

Jack stared back into that face, his brain seeking to match the visual with the impossible. He'd faced many situations in his time, but nothing like this.

For there, struggling beneath his grasp, was the resurrected form of Jim Rowston.

*   *   *

'I'm sorry if I gave you and your wife a scare, Jack.'

Cradling a mug of hot coffee and wiping some of the Fellows' best soil from his grimy face, Jim was clearly sorry for the horror he'd caused.

'Terrified us, more like.' Facing their uninvited guest across the kitchen table while Spike stretched out beneath, Jack and Audrey were calming their own shattered nerves with something stronger than coffee.

'But we thought you were dead,' explained Audrey as the brandy took effect. 'Everyone *said* you were.'

'Including me, because this morning I was told they'd found your body on board *Osprey*,' added Jack, not sure whether to smile with relief or frown with anger. 'So, if it wasn't *your* body they took to the Norwich morgue, whose was it?'

The engineer stared into his coffee before looking up, his glazed eyes filling. 'My kid-brother, Greg.'

Jack's eyes narrowed as realisation dawned. 'So, was it him you'd been going to see in Yarmouth?'

'Yes.'

'So, why the secrecy?'

'Because Greg's ... on the run.'

'From the police?'

'Yes. He'd been about to face trial for drug dealing, and then skipped bail.'

'So, he'd gone to ground in a holiday resort where he wouldn't be noticed amongst all the trippers and visitors,' surmised Jack.

'That's right, but also with a seaport and the added chance of finding a ship out of the country. He texted me asking for help with my old shipping contacts.'

'But no luck?'

'I didn't even try, Jack. I've stuck my neck out for my brother too many times over the years.'

'Including you getting caught up in drugs yourself, Jim, all that time ago?'

The engineer nodded and hung his head. 'Greg was always getting into scrapes, but they got more serious as he got older. I knew *how* serious when he contacted me while I was Second Engineer on a ship to the Far East. Apparently, he'd got the wrong side of a drug-dealing cartel and was threatened with his life if he didn't find a way to ship some cocaine out of that country. Greg led me to believe that if I didn't help, I was as good as signing his death warrant. I've never known my brother seem so terrified, so I stupidly agreed. They must have been a well-organised gang because, somehow, they managed to get the stuff onto my ship. My job was to land it at this end, so I concealed it in some engine parts going for overhaul. So much for my criminal expertise though. Sniffer dogs got straight onto it, I was arrested and ... you know the rest.'

'But you never let on the *real* story?'

'Couldn't do, Jack. Greg's bad-luck story was all a lie anyway to rope me in, but he'd already had so many run-ins with the law that a drugs offence would have seen him locked up for good.'

'So, you took the rap instead?'

'Yep. I'd been naive enough to be conned into getting involved in the first place, had let down my ship and company, and figured I deserved to be punished.'

'A pretty hefty price to pay, Jim, but it doesn't seem to have changed your brother's ways.'

'Nope. If anything he's gone off the rails even more since then, resulting in him getting arrested, charged and jumping bail. I found him sleeping rough under the pier at Yarmouth, so I booked him into a local B&B to get him cleaned up while I sorted out the best way ahead. Not that I'm on film star wages myself. In the end, I didn't even have the cash to pay for another night's lodging. And then Ralph Lampeter died and ...'

'... you took advantage of *Osprey* being left in your hands to give your brother a free berth on board,' finished off Jack.

'Yes. At the time it seemed a stroke of luck.' Jim gave an ironic laugh. 'How wrong can you be?'

'What happened exactly?'

'I wish I knew.' Jim shook his head in despair. 'We'd both eaten on board and then hit the sack. Greg was in the cabin Mr Lampeter had used and I kipped in my own. But, just after midnight, I heard a groan and heavy breathing. I dashed to see if he was okay, but got there only in time to hold his hand before he died.'

'You're sure he was dead?'

'Absolutely. I'd done the full Merchant Navy medical course and knew what to look for.'

'And your brother hadn't had any of Ralph's whisky?'

'No. I felt guilty enough just having him onboard, and gave him strict orders not to touch a thing that wasn't ours. And, anyway, the whisky wasn't there.'

'... because the police had taken it away for forensic testing. How about drugs, though – was your brother a user?'

'No, I'm pretty sure he was clean.'

'And you didn't think to call 999?'

Jim shook his head. 'I could have, but nothing would bring Greg back and my own record meant I wouldn't be getting a lot of understanding. I knew for sure I was on shaky ground.'

'You still are,' warned Jack. 'Apart from assisting a fugitive, failing to report a death is a pretty serious offence. So, why did you come here?'

'Because I thought you might help. I'd been stupid yet again, and running away like that wasn't going to help my case. You told me you'd been in the Met, and I had your address so ...'

'... here you are,' said Jack, giving a resigned sigh. 'All right, I'll help you, Jim, but only through legal channels. Luckily I know the investigating officer and I'll make sure he's aware that you came here tonight of your own free will. That might help, but accept the fact you're going to spend the next few nights in a cell again, and perhaps a few more after that.'

'Anything's better than all this hiding, Jack.'

'But what I don't understand,' joined in Audrey, getting up to find something to eat, 'is how they thought it was *you* who'd died on the boat.'

Jim shrugged. 'Greg was a couple of years younger than me, but in looks we were dead ringers. And we'd kept a low profile in the boatyard, because I didn't want anyone to know he was on board, so ...'

'... when one of the yard-hands came looking for you and found a body, he just assumed it was you,' completed Jack. 'And, of course, none of the police response team had ever seen you before either. I can see how it happened, Jim, but you certainly gave us a scare.'

'Yes, I'm truly sorry for that, but I'm so glad I came. I trust you to do the right thing.'

As Jack went to the phone and dialled Bailey's number, he hoped it wasn't a trust misplaced.

*　　*　　*

Chapter Ten

'So different to the Broads, but lovely just the same,' enthused Audrey, thoroughly enjoying the ride out.

It was next morning and the Fellows were already nearing the area reckoned to be the most likely for Margo's landscape. Though only thirty miles from home, this coastal fringe of North Norfolk, with its stunning, undulating countryside and occasional tantalising glimpses of glistening sea, was indeed very different to Broadland, and with a charm all of its own. And not one unappreciated by Spike on the back seat who, sensing they had almost arrived, was already panting with pent-up excitement.

'Yep, another little bit of Heaven-on-Earth.' At the wheel, Jack looked up into a blue sky clouded only by lingering cumulus to seaward. 'And a good day to enjoy some fresh sea air.'

'Which is more than poor Jim's doing this morning,' said Audrey, sadly. 'The poor chap, stuck now in a police cell, mourning his dead brother, and probably wondering what the future holds.'

'A few days of questioning at least.'

Bailey and uniformed officers had quickly responded to Jack's last-night call, taken Jim into custody and left the Fellows trying to reason this latest turn of events. 'I spoke to Bailey before we came out,' said Jack. 'I can't say he's that thrilled with the way things have turned out, but I think he's at least accepted that Jim gave himself up voluntarily.'

'And surely the courts will take that into consideration, won't they Jack, as well as the fact that, all along, he'd only been trying to help his brother?'

'I wouldn't bank on it.' Jack was turning left at the roundabout in Sheringham town and away from the coast road they'd been following. 'It doesn't help his case that there was another suspicious death on *Osprey* only a couple of days before. The law doesn't usually believe in coincidence and Jim's going to have to do some hard talking to get that one off his back.'

'Well, it *can't* be a coincidence,' reasoned Audrey. 'They must be linked in some way.'

'I'm sure you're right, Aud, but I'm still struggling to see how.'

'But you do think that both men were murdered?'

'No I don't, actually, but their deaths were certainly connected. The question is, how? In Greg's case, it can't have been the whisky, because the police had already taken it away for examination.'

'But Greg did use Ralph's cabin. Perhaps it was something in there.'

'Yeah, but Lampeter was in the saloon, so whatever killed *him* could have been anywhere on the boat.'

They were clear of Sheringham town now, breasting a hill before turning right into the park itself.

'What about carbon monoxide poisoning or fumes coming from the engine room?' suggested Audrey, as they wound along the short track to the car park.

'In which case, how come others weren't affected? Laura had spent at least five nights on the boat and Jim was on board when his brother died, but hadn't suffered any ill-effects himself.' Jack pulled into a grassy slot and switched off. 'Anyway, enough of that for the moment. We have another job to do.'

'Right, you go and get the ticket, while I sort Spike.'

By the time Jack returned, Audrey had the excited collie straining on his lead in one hand and their binoculars in the other. 'You'll probably need these.'

'Good thinking.'

They set off down the main trail bordered by many varieties of rhododendrons and azaleas and with breath-taking views of the estate's thousand acres opening up before them.

'You've certainly chosen a good time for this investigation, Jack,' enthused Audrey, stopping to sample the sweet fragrance of an azalea. 'The colours are out of this world.'

'Except we're here for more important issues,' chided Jack, pressing on down the slope that led, eventually, past Sheringham Hall and along a narrower trail to where a steel-framed tower rose above the enveloping canopy.

Audrey took one look at the steep path leading up to it and the two-hundred or so steps to the top. 'Perhaps you'd better go up alone, Jack. I'll stay here and look after Spike.'

'Probably best.' Jack unfolded the colour printout of the photo he'd taken of Margo's landscape, hitched the binoculars more securely over his shoulder and set off up.

Climbing upwards, perhaps a little slower than when he'd chased villains through London's East End, he finally reached the top, pausing only momentarily before orientating the printout to the amazing view the gazebo offered. At first, all looked the same as Margo's painting. Then, just as he was wondering if Audrey was right in thinking this might all be a waste of time and effort, he spotted something strangely out of context. With the binoculars, he studied this particular spot in even greater detail. Yes, he was correct. After marking it carefully on the map, he headed back down, grinning widely and giving his wife a satisfied thumbs-up as he neared the bottom.

'Obviously you found what you were looking for.'

'Actually, I *couldn't* find what I was looking for,' said Jack, contrarily, 'but that's just what I was hoping for.'

'Too early in the morning for riddles, Jack. What couldn't you find?'

'This.' Jack was jabbing his finger on the printout. 'Can you see what it is?'

Audrey popped on her specs. 'Do you mean the old mileage marker she's shown on the side of that narrow lane, right by those woods?'

'Exactly. There must be thousands of those century-old stone mileage markers up and down the country, but usually only on major highways, and there certainly isn't one on that lane now.'

'Perhaps there was when she did the painting, but they've got rid of it since.'

'Why would they? Those road-signs are part of our heritage, Aud. They never get rid of them. No, there never was one there in the first place.'

'Unless it *is* there, but now it's overgrown.'

'I doubt it, but we'll go and check.' Jack stuffed the printout back into his pocket, noticing as he did so, Spike looking back up at him with pleading eyes. 'It'll be a good place anyway to give this old boy a run off the lead. I think we're getting somewhere at last, Aud. We'll have a meal to celebrate on the way home, but first let's check that spot. Come on.'

Wife and collie could only follow on the uphill stretch back to the car, Spike looking forward to his free run and Audrey, a welcome meal after all this exercise.

*　　*　　*

'Well, you were right,' conceded Audrey, as they drove back towards Broadland. 'Not a road marker in sight anywhere.'

'And I knew there wouldn't be.' Jack gave the wheel a thump of satisfaction. 'We shouldn't underestimate that Margo, the crafty little madam.'

'But she only painted a small sign, Jack. Perhaps she was just using a bit of artistic licence to inject some period charm into her work?'

'Or for a rather more practical reason, if what I suspect is correct,' said Jack, enigmatically, before glancing at the dashboard clock. 'Twenty minutes to Sutton Staithe Hotel. It'll be good to eat there again.'

'It'll be lovely, Jack,' said Audrey, 'but any special reason we're returning to the same place we ate at just a few days ago?'

'Just good food and drink ... and something else I want to check up on.'

Audrey rolled cynical eyes. 'I might have known you'd have some ulterior motive, Jack Fellows. Okay, but on the way you can at least finish that account you were giving me last night before Jim's spooky arrival.'

'About my chat with Helen and Charles?'

'That's right ... Laura's heartbreak ... you never got around to giving me the details.'

'A bit of a strange story, actually.' Jack related the full account of Laura's lost love.

'More sad than "strange", Jack. It sounds simply a case of misguided love, but with a tragic ending.'

'Yes, but there are still parts that don't add up, Aud.'

'Such as?'

'For a start, why did Ralph and Charles go to the trouble of calling in the police and filing theft charges against this Peter Warmstead? Surely that goes completely against Ralph Lampeter's philosophy of giving offenders a second chance ... by doing just the opposite and turning a previously innocent lad *into* an offender?'

'Yes, that does seem odd,' agreed Audrey, 'but there is another factor here, Jack.'

'Which is?'

'That he was very much against this young man going out with his daughter. Fathers can be terribly protective when it comes to boyfriends, and Peter Warmstead being charged with theft would certainly hammer home *his* *un*suitability.'

'Good point, but another thing that bothers me is that Warmstead cleared off to India of all places. That's a long way to go, Aud, just to avoid a court case. Where did someone who needed to steal cash get the funds for a trip like that? It would cost thousands, so he must've got money from somewhere?'

'Could he have been sponsored by the organisation he ended up working for?'

'Not without references, he wouldn't be, or at such short notice.'

'Then perhaps this wasn't actually his first offense. Perhaps he'd got away with other thefts and had a bit stashed away.' Audrey gave a sad smile. 'Anyway, the poor lad paid a high price, being killed like that by a terrorist bomb.'

'*But*, while working on relief projects,' pointed out Jack, 'which doesn't sound the sort of voluntary venture a chap with criminal tenancies would take on. And Helen gave me the impression *she* liked him, so he obviously came across as a likeable lad.'

'And I would've thought Laura was more discerning,' agreed Audrey. 'Anyway, the whole business must've been devastating for her. No wonder she's had nothing to do with men ever since.'

'I'm not so sure of that either.'

'What do you mean?'

'That I get the impression that this "friend" she keeps going to stay with in Norwich might actually be a bit more than that.'

'You mean a new boyfriend? What gives you that idea?'

'Just that she would've used a name by now, but all she ever refers to is "her friend", leaving us to assume it's a female, but telling me it's a bloke she wants to keep under wraps.'

'And who can blame her for being cautious, after what happened the last time, Jack.'

'Yeah, I can understand her keeping it from her father, but he's dead now and I'm sure her mum would be thrilled to see her in a new relationship. We'll soon find out though, because Bailey's checking everyone's alibi and Laura will have to be completely honest with him.' Jack gave his stomach a pat. 'Anyway, not far to go now. I'm ready for lunch. All that fresh air has given me an appetite.'

*   *   *

'I'll have steak and kidney pie, and my wife, the scampi.' Order placed and with Spike snoring quietly under the table, Jack sat back contentedly and raised his glass of lager. 'Good health, love, and here's to investigations.'

'Just as long as they're all worthwhile and we get to enjoy perks like this,' agreed Audrey, taking in the friendly atmosphere surrounding their corner table just off the public bar. 'So much nicer without all the hidden undercurrents we were putting up with the last time we were here.' She took a sip of her wine. 'Mmm, perfect, and a large one too.'

'You've earned it, Aud. This whole business has been a bit of a nightmare for both of us.'

'And it's still a complete mystery to me, Jack.' Audrey shook her head. 'I've never known a case with so many disjointed aspects, what with steamboat disasters, ghostly visitations, estranged couples, adulterous wives, broken romances, questionable boat deals, not to mention an unexplained death and murder.'

'Yeah, bit of a tangle isn't it,' agreed Jack. 'I have to admit, it's had me scratching my head. A bit like one of those children's drawing books where you have to join up the dots, but, in this case, without the benefit of numbers. The trick, I've found, is to stop taking events at face value, and instead try and see them through the eyes of others.'

'I dread to think what you might see through the eyes of Margo.' Audrey pulled a face. 'Surely the fact that her prints were found on *Osprey* the night of Ralph's death and her car was seen driving away, puts her well and truly in the frame.'

'But with what motive?'

'I can think of some, Jack. From the heated conversation we overheard in the Secret Garden, there was obviously a lot of bad feeling brewing up between the two of them. Perhaps, when Margo visited at midnight, it all escalated into a blazing row. Hell knows no fury ... and all that. She probably knew about Ralph's medication and, when his back was turned, added some to his whisky out of sheer spite.'

'So, why would she put some in the bottle as well if it wasn't premeditated?' reasoned Jack. 'And how do you account for Greg Rowston's death, because we know the police had already taken that bottle away before he ever went on board?'

'Okay,' reconsidered Audrey, 'but there must be some connection between the two. Perhaps it really is Jim.'

'A logical conclusion, I grant you, but it doesn't gel with what I think is the real truth behind this whole business.'

'Which is?'

'Something I've yet to prove ... but over there is someone who might provide the answer,' said Jack, seeing a waitress he recognised. 'She's the one I settled our bill with last Saturday.'

'So, how on earth can she help, Jack?'

'You'd be surprised.'

He called her over and she remembered their last meeting. 'Not a problem with the bill I hope?'

'Not with *ours*, but I've been worrying there was something the group didn't pay for. Have you still got the original bill?'

'Yes, I'll go and get it.' She soon returned with the printout.

Jack took his time scrutinising the long list of meals and drinks before spotting the item he wanted. 'Ah yes, there it is. We did pay for it after all.'

With the waitress thanked and off back to her dining room, Audrey looked more puzzled than ever. 'What did you think hadn't been paid for?'

'Oh, yet another piece of the jigsaw, Aud, but an important one for completing the picture.'

Audrey sighed. 'Pictures are what this mystery seems to be all about.' She leaned a little closer to her husband. 'So when can the rest of us see it?'

'Just as soon as I can fit in the two final pieces.'

'So, do you know who the murderer is?'

'I do now, Aud, but I can't say until I've got it totally figured out.'

Audrey sat back, frustrated. 'So what about all these clues you *have* figured out? Don't they count for anything?'

'Only to show what a clever murderer we're dealing with here. I'm pretty sure of the motive now, but still stumped for means *or* opportunity.'

'I wish I could help more,' sympathised Audrey. She looked around at the friendly ambience of the bar. 'Hard to think it's less than a week since we were all here having a meal together. You and I don't get to go to a restaurant very often these days.'

'Well, here come our meals, so make the most of it.'

They were soon tucking in, though Audrey could tell her husband's mind was elsewhere. 'Penny for them, Jack.'

It was a second before Jack realised he was being spoken to. 'What? ... sorry?'

'Something's just occurred to you, hasn't it?'

'Oh, just that remark you made about restaurants. It linked two other, seemingly, innocent bits of information I already had.'

'I was only really thinking how much had happened since we were last here,' said Audrey, not even attempting to fathom other obscure reasoning. 'And then the next day we were at How Hill eavesdropping on Ralph and Margo's fallout. I can't believe we did that, and in such a beautiful setting ... all those unusual plants and your story about the tree stump with the sailing boat carving on it.'

'Oh, you mean the remains of the oak tree given at the Berlin Olympics?'

'That's the one.' Audrey sighed. 'It's funny how even trees can have a bad association.' But, even as she said it, she could see another spark of enlightenment in her husband's eyes. 'I've done it again haven't I, Jack? You've just thought of something else.'

'Yes, what you said about trees, coupled to that one about restaurants.'

'What have either of those two unrelated and innocent remarks to do with anything?'

'*A lot*, Aud, if what I'm thinking isn't totally bonkers.' Meals almost eaten, Jack was clearly impatient to get going. 'When you're done, I need to get home to check some facts.'

'So much for our relaxing meal,' groaned Audrey, pushing away her plate. 'I should have known better than to even mention this past week.'

'I'm glad you did, Aud, because you've probably just given me the means. All we need now is the opportunity and we've got it cracked.'

*   *   *

It was ten o'clock that night before Jack managed to get Bailey on his home number. The DI sounded both tired and not at his most tolerant.

'Strewth, Jack, what time do you call this? I've only just got in. Don't you have a bed of your own to go to?'

'Yes, after I've had an update from you on autopsies, Bailey. I'm assuming they've also done Greg Rowston's by now.'

'Yes, I pushed for it, with his death so suspiciously soon after the other. A bit disappointing though.'

'In what way?'

'Just that it was as inconclusive as Lampeter's. Both men certainly died from heart failure, but probably from natural causes.'

'In other words, the toxicology tests didn't bring up anything?'

'Only that Lampeter had a fair amount of *digitalis* in his system, but only enough appropriate for a man taking it anyway as medication.'

'But his tumbler of whisky dregs were laced with the stuff, as was the bottle behind the bar,' pointed out Jack, 'so it certainly looked like someone wanted him snuffed. How about Greg Rowston?'

'Completely negative for *digitalis*. A pity, because a link between those two deaths would have put brother Jim well into the frame.'

'Why?'

'Because he's the only one connected to both victims, Jack. As it is, Greg's death will probably go down as "natural causes".'

'Which it wasn't,' persisted Jack, 'because Jim reckons his brother was a fit young man.'

'As confirmed by his autopsy,' agreed Bailey.

'I do have another suggestion,' offered Jack. 'I've just been doing a bit of research myself, and there's something else I'd like the toxicologists to check.'

'"Something else"! We can't look as though we're telling them how to do their job, Jack.'

'We can if it's something they might never have heard of before. Copy this down, Bailey, and see what they say.'

'I'll do my best, but I'm not promising.' After wearily taking down the data Jack gave him, the DI had at least one item of positive news. 'I did manage to get that other information you wanted, though. It took a morning of phone calls to some pretty improbable places, so I hope it helps.' Bailey read out his findings. 'Goodness knows where that fits into anything, but I'm sure you'll let me know if it does.'

'Perhaps sooner than you think,' assured Jack. 'That's made a lot of things possible and even probable if these next tests come up positive, but I do need another favour, Bailey. You remember I promised to get Ralph Lampeter's things off the boat for the family? Well, with all the shock of that other death I completely forgot. Can I get them now?'

'Are they that important?'

'They might be ... but for us more than them.'

'Okay. Our boys have got all they want. I've got Rowston's key, but there's a spare with the yard office, so I'll call them and authorise you to use that.'

'Thanks, Bailey. I owe you a drink.'

'That's what you always say, Jack,' declared the DI, laughing, 'but it'll be a while now before I have another evening off. Are you free tomorrow lunchtime so we can compare notes?'

'I'll be on duty, but you sound like you could do with some fresh air. I'll be patrolling the Ant again, so how about we meet up on Irstead staithe?'

'You're on. See you then.'

With the DI off salvaging what was left of his evening, Jack joined Audrey for their nightcap in the lounge.

'For goodness' sake, come and sit down and relax for just a few minutes,' she scolded. 'I don't know about you, Jack, but I'm ready for bed.'

'Yeah, it'll be good to hit the sack,' agreed Jack. He sighed. 'The trouble with getting older, Aud, is that even going to bed these days seems to involve a whole checklist of things to do first ... pills to pop, eye-drops to put in, and that's even before you ...' But, once again, Jack had trailed off mid-sentence.

'"Before you" ... what, Jack?'

'Before the clever way I reckon Ralph Lampeter got prematurely shoved off his mortal coil. That's it, Aud. I think we've just cracked the "opportunity".'

*   *   *

119

Chapter Eleven

Jack was sad to see *Osprey* already showing signs of neglect next morning as, once more, he slid his launch alongside the Ludham Bridge boatyard. Without Jim's dedicated hand, the old boat's brasswork was becoming dull, and her normally glistening white upper-works streaked with rivulets of dirt and grime. Adding to this air of abandonment, the police CRIME SCENE tapes were still entwined about the boat like some badly-wrapped and unwanted present. After collecting the keys from the yard office, Jack was soon ducking under them, the gloomy morning not easing his sombre mood.

Perhaps it was because he had known the old steamboat in happier times. That was less than a week ago, but there was now an eerie feel about the vessel as she creaked at her mooring lines in the freshening breeze. Certainly the saloon's snug atmosphere had been replaced by the cold chill of death, with Ralph Lampeter's armchair still carrying the imprint of his corpse and the small table beside it, the stains of his final drink. Thrown carelessly across an adjoining couch was the blanket Jack had used to cover his body. He picked it up again now, refolded it and made his way for'ard.

This was the first time he'd been in the owner's cabin since Lampeter's murder. Since then it had only been used by Jim's late brother Greg, and there was still some evidence of the young man's brief and fatal stay. Lying scattered about were items of discarded clothing and just a few meagre possessions, including a battered old rucksack. Jack went through its pockets. If his hunch was correct, there was something he wouldn't find here ... and he didn't. Satisfied at that, he quickly collected the few personal items of Ralph's that still remained, bundled them into a leather holdall bearing the deceased's embossed initials, and left.

Back in his launch and turning upriver for his meeting with Bailey, Jack breathed down a good lungful of Broadland air. The deaths on *Osprey* had been the result of a well thought-out plot. Hopefully, the additional data he'd asked the DI for would help him prove it.

*   *   *

Thankfully, Irstead Staithe was empty of boats when Jack came gliding into this tranquil mooring, the previous night's occupants long gone and the forthcoming ones, yet to arrive.

But Bailey was already there waiting, standing beside his car and seemingly soaking up an atmosphere very different to his usual one in CID. As Jack secured the launch, the DI came wandering across the green, raising his collar against the chill wind. 'Even without the sun, Jack, I have to say I prefer your office to mine.'

'I know what you mean, Bailey. Come on board.'

The two men settled into the aft cockpit, the trees around them swaying and rustling in the breeze while the launch pulled at her lines. Jack produced a thermos of coffee from his bag. 'First things first.'

'Thanks.' Bailey took the offered cup. 'Hopefully, this might help get my few remaining brain cells working.'

Jack nodded. 'Bit of a teaser, this one, isn't it?'

'In so many ways, Jack. I'd been pretty sure of nailing Jim Rowston for double murder by *digitalis* poisoning. Now I'm back to square one.'

'Not if these other tests prove positive. How are they doing?'

'Slowly, seeing as it's something they haven't encountered before. This substance doesn't show up on normal toxicology tests and finding it is going to involve liquid chromatography coupled with mass spectrometry ... or so they tell me.' The DI raised his eyes to the heavens. 'The Chief Constable's going to go apoplectic when he gets the bill. By this time next year I'll probably be back on point duty.'

'Or promoted.' Jack delved back into his bag. 'Anyway, here's something else for those boffins to test.'

'For the same thing?'

'Yep, so don't try using it yourself.'

'Don't worry, I won't,' said Bailey, popping the item into an evidence bag, 'but this might take another day or so, Jack.'

'It'll be worth it. In the meantime, are you still holding Rowston?'

'Too right I am. Sheltering an offender and failing to report a death is enough, but he's still my number one suspect for murder.'

'I think you're wasting your time there, Bailey. Right now you'd be better off getting West Midlands police to pay a little visit to a certain business in their patch.' Jack handed the DI a handwritten address.

'Is it connected to this case?'

'Not directly, but I reckon it'll still be worthwhile.' Jack sipped his coffee. 'How about everyone's alibi for last Sunday? What did you find out there?'

Bailey went through their findings, but pointed out one name specifically. 'You'll remember that one from the other obscure information I got for you the other day.'

'Yeah, and I'm not surprised. Any chance of a photo to match it?'

'I can try the national papers. They might have one in their archives.'

'That'd be great, especially if you can email it to me tonight.'

Bailey sighed. 'I'll do my best, Jack, if you think it important.'

'I do. Things are coming to a head now, Bailey and we need to act.'

'Any ideas how?'

'Same as we've done before, but while the iron's still hot. I'm off duty tomorrow, so how about we call a meeting of everyone for the afternoon.'

'Won't that put the frights up whoever it is we're trying to nail here?'

'Not if we wrap it up as some sort of social gathering. The rally kind of fizzled out after Lampeter's death, so how about I get Laura to call everyone for a *Steambuffs* get-together before they all go their separate ways?'

'Sounds a good idea, but where do you propose to hold this jolly?'

'It needs to be somewhere relaxed. The rally started at the Museum of the Broads, so how about there for late afternoon when all the visitors have left? One person we need to have included though is Jim Rowston.'

'Okay, Jack, I'll let him out, but there'll be some of my men close by just in case.'

'We'll want them there anyway, if this works out as I hope, but also try and hurry up those toxicology experts. That evidence will be vital to get this case wrapped.'

'That's one thing I can't promise,' warned Bailey, handing back his empty mug. 'Call me tonight, Jack, to confirm.'

The two men went their separate ways, the DI back to his world of crime and Jack to his of remote waters, open skies and people free to enjoy it.

Hopefully, tomorrow would help keep it that way.

*   *   *

'Was that DI Bailey you were just calling?' asked Audrey late that evening as Jack finally joined her and Spike in the lounge.

'Yep, I was just thanking him for a photo he'd emailed me ... that and confirming Laura had managed to get all the rally members together for tomorrow afternoon's supposed social.'

'That must have taken some organising.'

'I'm sure it did, but she was more than happy to arrange it, seeing as she thought it was a good suggestion anyway. And the museum's agreed to hire us the café area for a couple of hours after the public closing time.'

'I'm glad Laura likes the idea,' said Audrey, 'but how about the other members?'

'Apparently, degrees of enthusiasm from some,' acknowledged Jack, going to the sideboard and pouring himself a stiff drink. 'Most seemed glad of the chance to chat things over, though I gather some grumbled it was a waste of their time.'

'I can imagine who they were.'

Jack plonked down into his favourite chair, gave Spike a loving head-stroke, and stretched his legs. 'Yeah, well, whoever "they" are, they may well find it's more than a couple of hours that Her Majesty demands of their time after tomorrow.'

'Oh dear, sounds like it's going to be stressful meeting,' frowned Audrey. 'All the more important that you try and relax tonight. How about watching something on TV before bed?'

'I'd planned on doing that anyway ... the coverage of the first day of the rally at the museum you recorded for me, but which I never did get round to watching.'

'I was thinking of something a bit more light-hearted to take your mind off steamboats for *one* evening, Jack. Any particular reason you want to see it now?'

'I just want to check something, which is also the reason I'm off to Norwich again in the morning.'

'Not *another* visit, Jack. Is all this really necessary?'

'It is if it helps catch a murderer.'

Audrey, put down her knitting. 'You really are sure it was murder then, Jack?'

'Absolutely, *and* who did it. As always, though, the hard part is *proving* it. Bailey's still not got the extra toxicology test results back, and without those we're on shaky ground for making an arrest.'

'So why not put off the meeting?'

'Because we need to get this wrapped up, Aud, and even if we don't have everything tomorrow, there should be enough proof to take the accused into custody pending other charges.'

'Do you really have enough evidence for that?'

'I think so, as long as we can get those involved turning on each other.'

'My goodness,' said Audrey, shaking her head, 'who'd have thought a fun weekend on the Broads could become so acrimonious.'

'Yeah, but all this criminality and hate had been brewing for years, Aud. It only needed a spark to set off the chain reaction and, sadly, the rally provided it. The important thing now is to bring justice to those that deserve it.'

'Yes, well I just hope you know what you're doing,' warned Audrey. 'And where exactly do we need to go in Norwich tomorrow?'

'The Great Hospital.'

'Oh good, I always enjoy going there.'

'Actually, I was planning on going alone, Aud ...' Jack cast his wife a nervous glance, '... because there was something else I was hoping you'd do in the morning.'

'Really, what's that?'

'Bake us some cakes for the meeting.' He knocked back the rest of his drink. 'May as well make it as pleasant as we can before the accusations begin.'

*   *   *

Chapter Twelve

'Now I know how Daniel must've felt going into the lion's den,' said Audrey late the next day as she and Jack entered the museum enclosure. In the freshening wind, the canvas awning above was lifting and cracking while the bunting from the previous Saturday's open-day still fluttered bravely, as though forlornly trying to inject a bit of levity into this latest event.

'Don't worry, Aud.' Jack raised the plates of newly-baked chocolate and blueberry muffins he was carrying. 'These'll put everyone at their ease.'

'I think it'll take more than those to soften the blow once some of them realise your full agenda, Jack ... especially when they see *he's* also been invited,' added Audrey, spotting DI Bailey lurking behind the hull of an old river-inspectors' launch.

'Hopefully, with some good news.' Jack handed over the goodies. 'You take these in, Aud, while I go and have a quick word.'

Unfortunately, Bailey's words were not what Jack had hoped for. 'Sorry, mate, but I've let you down on this one. I just checked with HQ and they still haven't got that extra toxicology report.'

'Ah, a pity, because I was banking on that.' Jack shrugged away the setback. 'Right, we'll just have to make do with what we've got.' He glanced around. 'Have you got some men handy?'

Bailey nodded in the direction of the public staithe. 'Keeping a low profile over there and just standing by in case they're needed.'

'Let's hope they will be.' Jack led the DI inside. It was time to make themselves unpopular.

*   *   *

In the museum café area, the rally members were warming up to the occasion and beginning to enjoy at least the semblance of a social atmosphere. Surrounded by Broadland memorabilia, and with Audrey's cakes now being washed down with a glass or two of wine, there was much chatter, not least, about the happenings in the days since they'd last met. Conversation did, perhaps, abate slightly when they saw who Jack had just walked in with, but resumed as Laura broke away from her mum and went to greet him.

'Jack ... good to see you ... and you, Inspector.' She nodded towards the assembly. 'This was a good idea of yours. We needed to have a happier ending to the rally after all that's happened ...' she turned back to Bailey, '... though I wasn't expecting you, Inspector. Not a formal visit, I hope?'

'Actually, we do want to talk to everyone,' said Bailey.

'To update you all on progress so far,' added Jack, quickly checking everyone from the rally really was here.

Certainly Doctor Edwards and Lionel Hillbeck were deep in conversation, while their wives and Audrey had formed a chatting threesome further down the room. Helen Lampeter, after giving Jack a welcoming wave, had moved to rejoin Charles Seager as he in turn sought to extricate himself from the ever-tedious Harry Bryant. Over by the wherry cabin, Jim Rowston was looking somewhat subdued and uncomfortable, though Jack was pleased to see Dexter had made the effort to take him a drink and that they were now conversing affably, doubtless about their joint love of *Osprey*. Only Margo Berrington stood alone, perhaps the most fashionably dressed female in the room, but certainly not the most popular. Going by the contemptuous looks she was throwing the others, it was a feeling reciprocated.

'Okay, I'll just say a few words of welcome,' said Laura, breaking into Jack's surveillance, 'and then hand over to you.' She tapped her glass for silence. 'Hello everyone, good to see you all here. A lot's happened since we first set sail on this rally ...' she paused for a unanimous murmur of sympathetic agreement, '... but Jack here has come to update us on what's been going on as a result of two very sad and tragic deaths.' She stood to one side. 'Jack.'

'Thanks, Laura.' As everyone made themselves comfortable at the scattered tables, Jack made a quick appraisal of facial expressions. Perhaps a couple appeared less than enthusiastic, but most looked eager to find out what this was all about. They wouldn't have to wait long, because he'd already decided this was no time to pull punches.

'As you all know, last Saturday night one of your long-time members, Ralph Lampeter, died unexpectedly on his boat. Or, to be more precise, he was murdered, and by someone sitting here right now.'

Jack had intended to shock and, judging by the sharp intakes of breath and gasps, he'd succeeded. As most cast nervous glances at their neighbours, it was Charles Seager who decided to intervene.

'Do you have proof of that, Fellows?'

'Some, yes, and plenty of circumstantial evidence, the most significant being that none of you here actually liked Ralph Lampeter, and quite a few

126

had reason to rejoice at his sudden demise.'

'I hope you're not going to start accusing anyone,' declared Seager, in his best lawyer manner, 'but if you are, then how about *him*?' He was pointing to Jim Rowston, still standing beside the wherry cabin. 'We all know about his time in prison, and *he's* the only one with connections to both deaths.'

Jim unfolded his arms and stepped forward, scowling. 'My brother's death was just a sad accident, and why would I want to harm Mr Lampeter, a man I respected and who gave me a chance to rebuild my life?'

'Actually, that's not strictly true, is it, Jim?' refuted Jack, turning to the engineer, 'because you knew all along that Ralph wasn't the upstanding person he pretended to be. Secretly despising him for it, you avoided having much contact while looking after *Osprey*, and told me you had no intention of taking up the other work he'd offered when the boat was sold. I think I know why, but I also know it wasn't you who murdered your boss.' He turned back to Seager. 'But I *am* going to point fingers, Charles, and let's start with you.'

'Me?'

'Yes. I don't think it's any secret that you and Helen here have had a long and close relationship, want to marry, but been thwarted by the deceased's refusal to agree to a divorce. That alone was conveniently solved by his death.'

'Rubbish!' It was Helen, speaking up and clearly stung by Jack's insinuation. 'I thought you knew me better than that, Jack. I might have hated Ralph for it, but I certainly wouldn't want him dead.'

'But it was more than about a simple divorce, wasn't it Helen?' pressed Jack. 'In truth, you had a much stronger motive for having him out of your life.'

'Which was?'

'Money. The romantics might have us believe that love makes the world go around, but a bit of cash certainly helps it on its way and you'd inherited a small fortune. As long as you and Ralph were still married, he had a claim to his share, and so he was making life difficult for you by holding out for a lucrative divorce settlement. Now, as a result of his death, you're not only free to marry Charles, but get to keep all of your inheritance ... and, of course, *Osprey*.'

'I can't believe you'd think that of my mother,' protested Laura. 'She wouldn't hurt a fly, let alone *kill* anyone.'

'You'd be surprised what people can do when the chips are down,' countered Jack. 'Even you, Laura. You knew the pain your father had put your mother through over the years. His affair with someone *you* once thought of as your best friend broke up their marriage, and he was still openly fraternising with that same woman in front of everyone at the rally, including her husband.'

'Do we have to go into that?' said Dexter, standing up. 'We all know you're talking about my wife, but is now the time and place?'

'It is if it's pertinent,' replied Jack, 'and what could be more so than a jealous husband seeking revenge?'

'Are you saying *I* killed Lampeter?' said Dexter in a threatening voice, his fists clenching into hard balls.

'Why not? You had motive *and* opportunity because you were sleeping alone in *Pickle* and close by, the night of the death. All you had to do was sneak along the moorings at midnight and ... problem solved.'

'You think so?' scoffed Dexter. 'Believe me, Jack, if I'd really wanted to kill Lampeter, I'd have broken his neck with my bare hands, not poisoned him.'

'Who said anything about poison?' asked Jack, suspiciously. 'That information hasn't been general knowledge ... or did Margo tell you?'

'Now hang on a minute.' True to form, Dexter wasn't going to stand by as the finger of suspicion came to rest on his wife. 'Are you now incriminating Margo, just on the strength of idle hearsay?'

'More than hearsay, Dexter. We have evidence *and* a witness that puts your wife on board *Osprey* the night Ralph Lampeter met his death.'

'Witness ... what witness?'

'Me, actually.' Doctor Edwards stepped forward. 'Sorry, Dexter, but I actually saw Margo driving away that night.'

'It can't have been her. She was at home in Norwich.'

'Oh, shut up, Dexter.' Margo's outburst startled everyone. She stood there for a second, blinked once, took a long drink of her wine and seemed to accept the inevitable. 'Okay, I admit it. I *was* there that night.'

'*What?*' Her husband seemed more shocked than anyone.

'Don't look so surprised, Dexter. You've known all along that there was something going on between me and Ralph. But, believe me, I didn't kill him.' Margo ran nervous fingers through her dark hair, and there was a slight tremor – real or affected – in her voice. 'Yes, I went to *Osprey* that night to try and get some money out of the old boy. I went straight down into the saloon and, there he was, sitting in his chair, dead as a dodo. It wasn't a nice experience, I can tell you. When I realised he wasn't simply asleep, I just panicked and fled.'

'Not quite like that was it, Mrs Berrington,' said Bailey, stepping forward. 'We have evidence that proves you actually spent some time drinking with the deceased.'

'I did *what?*' Margo looked genuinely puzzled.

'Yes, a half-drunk glass of wine with your fingerprints all over it, found right next to the victim's tumbler of whisky and containing a fatal dose of his prescription *digitalis*.'

'*Digi...* what?' Margo shook her head in apparent disbelief. 'That can't have been anything to do with me. I swear I didn't spend another second in that saloon after I found him like that ... and why would I want to kill him anyway?'

'Because you owed him money,' said Jack bluntly. 'Always a good motive for murder, Margo, but not only were you in debt to Ralph, you'd gone to *Osprey* that night to beg for even more.'

'And we can all guess what she was offering in return,' sneered Laura.

'How dare you?' Margo was doing her best to look affronted. 'What do you think I am?'

'We all *know* what you are, Margo,' answered Laura. 'It's just how low you're prepared to sink to get what you want that we're now finding out.'

'Chance would have been a fine thing. I tell you he was dead when I got there.'

'And so you just took off without even trying to summon help,' threw back Laura in disgust. 'That just about sums up the extent of your caring nature, you little bitch.'

'I ... I couldn't call anyone, could I?' stammered Margo. 'I was in ... in a ...'

'... compromising position?' completed Laura with contempt. 'No change there then, Margo.'

'Actually, they weren't *just* lovers,' intervened Jack. 'They were also involved in a business partnership.'

'Doing what?' asked a bemused Helen, 'and is it related to Ralph's murder?'

'Not directly, but it's a pretty sordid story that needs to be told if justice is to be done.' Jack cast an eye over the others sitting forward in expectation. 'And I guess now's the time to do just that.'

*   *   *

'You don't have stay for any of this, Margo.' Dexter had gone straight to his wife's side and put a firm hand on her shoulder. 'I think we should leave right now.'

'A good idea, Dex, but it doesn't look as if that's an option.' Margo was glancing at DI Bailey, who'd repositioned himself by the exit. She turned with resignation back to the others, all agog to hear what she had to say. 'Okay, I admit I haven't led a blameless life. Ralph and I first hit it off when Laura took me to her home for a weekend and ...' she shrugged, '... well, you can all probably guess the rest.'

Jack scanned the members, whose expressions showed they probably had.

'Unfortunately, handling things that weren't yours became a bit of a habit, didn't it, Margo? Because, not long after that, you started selling antiques to Ralph Lampeter?'

'That's right.' With the subject currently off murder, Margo was showing a little of her old feistiness. 'There's nothing wrong with that is there?'

'There is if they weren't yours to sell.' There was dead silence in the room and even Margo had gone pale as Jack fixed her with a hard stare. 'I was puzzled from the start how you, a young woman fresh out of art college, could straightway afford to buy your own gallery.'

'With an unexpected inheritance and by selling paintings and antiques,' protested Margo, turning back to the members and managing to force a smile.

'Well, you certainly cashed in on your painting and antique trading all right,' agreed Jack, 'but not in the way we might think, and certainly without help from a non-existent inheritance. Let me speculate on how I think it happened. It's going to sound far-fetched, but I bet I'm pretty close.'

'Go on then.'

'Okay, in my imagination I see you just after you've graduated, your friendship with Laura ended, and struggling to make a living painting local landscapes. The place you've chosen to paint from this day is the gazebo, the tall lookout tower at Sheringham Park, which certainly gives wonderful views of the surrounding countryside. I'm guessing it's early in the season when there aren't too many other visitors and you can paint in peace. Except, at some point, your attention's drawn to a man acting suspiciously beside a wood on a quiet lane just half a mile away. Through your binoculars you watch him bury something in the wood. Intrigued, you mark the spot on your painting and later go and check it out. Locating the newly turned earth, you dig down and find a sackful of valuable antiques.'

'Rubbish!'

Jack shook his head. 'No, not rubbish, Margo, but the spoils from a recent robbery at the nearby stately home of the Otterton family. But, far from reporting your find to the police, you saw it as a fast-track way into the world of antique dealing. After allowing a suitable period for the heat to die down, you began discreetly selling them off, many to Ralph Lampeter. Amongst other things, he bought a silver-plated coffee pot, which he thought would look good on *Osprey* because it was already engraved with the letter 'O'. It was on that boat until the night of the murder, but the next morning I noticed it was gone.'

Margo feigned a laugh. 'What are you saying? That I'd commit murder for the sake of a lousy coffee pot?'

'Of course not, but you realised the police would attend Ralph's death and that it might be recognised as stolen property. Such an expensive looking antique would certainly have stood out so, before fleeing the scene, you stuffed the pot into your bag, hoping it would avoid awkward questions later.' Jack gave a nod of admiration. 'Quick thinking, Margo, especially when you were dealing with a problem far worse.'

'Now what are you talking about?'

'The fact that the whole business had suddenly come back to haunt you ... including the thief you saw from the gazebo, burying his ill-gotten gains. Soon after that, he was arrested and jailed for possession, but those hidden antiques were never recovered and, after serving his time, he went to dig up his nest-egg and ... surprise, surprise ... found it gone. Fast forward now to last week and he finds himself browsing *ArtVu*'s window, sees your landscape of a place he recognises and instantly realises who'd nicked his loot.'

Jack could imagine the other *Steambuffs* finding all this a bit hard to take and wasn't surprised when Doctor Edwards spoke up. 'But, Jack, how would this thief *know* the picture was connected to his robbery?'

'Good point, Doctor but, recognising a familiar scene, the thief's eyes would have automatically gone to his chosen hiding place. But what he saw painted to mark it was something he knew wasn't there at the time.' Jack brought out the print of Margo's landscape, held it up and pointed. 'An old country milestone that she assumed would be in keeping with the scene and so not look out of place.'

For a change, Margo was speechless, but Charles had a question. 'So, did she recognise this man?'

'Very much so. It scared her to death and she must have been terrified when he later confronted her, demanding recompense.' Jack turned back to Margo. 'Things were turning nasty but, of course, you couldn't go to the police, so you had to pay up ... or at least Dexter did.'

'What bad luck though,' commented Pat Hillbeck, 'this thief just happening to spot her painting like that.'

'Not bad luck at all, actually,' explained Jack. 'You see, the thief was in Norwich for this rally and, presumably, just decided to look up Dexter Berrington to discuss buying *Pickle*. He must have thought all his Christmases had come at once when he realised the artist was the wife behind the counter.'

'You mean ...'

'Yep, that the thief's actually a member of *Steambuffs*, and is sitting here with us right now.'

'One of *us*?' Again, it was Charles voicing the shock felt by them all.

'I'm afraid so.' Jack glanced to the far end of the hall where one of their number was about to slide out through the exit. 'Going somewhere, Harry?'

Harry Bryant froze before trying a brave attempt at nonchalance. 'Just off to the loo.'

'You'll probably need it after you've heard what else I've got to say ...' Jack folded his arms, '... because it was you, wasn't it Harry, who'd burgled Otterton Hall all those years ago?'

'I don't know what you're talking about.'

'Yes you do, but it's your more recent crimes we need to discuss now.'

'What ... murder?' There was more than a hint of fear in Bryant's voice. 'You can't pin that on me.'

Bailey stepped forward. 'Perhaps not immediately, Harry, but there is something else that we can. Last night, West Midlands Police raided *Heritage Engineering*. Would you care to explain why they found those premises stuffed with stolen goods from stately homes and worth many thousands of pounds?'

'I ... I can't answer that,' stammered Bryant.

'Let me help you then,' offered Jack, 'because it confirms what I suspected all along.'

'Which was?'

'That employing ex-prisoners in your engineering business was just a cover for theft on a, literally, industrial scale.'

Helen seemed more shocked than anyone, and with good reason. 'But that must mean Ralph was in on it as well.'

'And much deeper than you can imagine, I'm afraid, Helen,' confirmed Jack. 'In fact, his *New Start* charity was actually the heart of a well-organised scam that's been operating for several years.'

'But how? ... why?'

'The same old reason ... money. I'm guessing that when RLC went bust, he needed to fill the void. His affair with Margo hadn't ended, and I suspect she told him about her stolen antiques and that she needed help shifting them. No doubt Ralph offered to do what he could, and I think it was this that gave him an idea. As he could no longer employ ex-offenders at RLC, why not create a charity to find them work elsewhere while also cashing in on their dubious talents? So, *New Start* was formed, on the surface, a well-respected organisation, but, in reality, an agency for house-breaking and burglary. He paid commission on results and Margo, living well out of the area, was perfectly placed to look after the distribution.'

Lionel Hillbeck shook his head in disbelief as the penny dropped. 'So Bryant's engineering business was a cover for all this criminal activity.'

'Very much so, as was *ArtVu* for Margo. I'm sure Harry will correct me if I'm wrong, but I'm guessing that, after doing his three years, he approached *New Start* for help and, with his background, Ralph decided to plough some of his rapidly accumulating profits into setting up *Heritage Engineering* as the perfect cover for expansion.'

'Of course, let me stress I was no longer associated with Ralph Lampeter after his business collapsed ...' interrupted Charles, keen to distance himself from any involvement.

'Hypocrite,' muttered Laura under her breath.

If Charles heard, he chose to ignore it and continued, '... but, anyway, I'm bloody sure, Fellows, that you don't have a shred of evidence to back up this ridiculous theory.'

'Not yet,' admitted Jack, 'but you remember me mentioning Jim Rowston's reluctance to work for Bryant if *Osprey* were sold. His actual words were that he'd "made a mistake once, but didn't intend to repeat it". Those words rang alarm bells and started me questioning what really lay behind *New Start*.'

'Which we now *know* was just a veneer of respectability screening a world of crime,' said Bailey as two constables made their appearance, 'so, Harry Bryant, I'm arresting you under suspicion of contravening the Serious Crime Act of 2007 by encouraging and inciting others to commit crime.'

As the DI read Bryant his rights and the other *Steambuffs* stared open-mouthed, Margo couldn't contain her relief at seemingly being out of the immediate frame. 'Serves the greedy bastard right for trying to blackmail me. He made poor Dexter here sign over *Pickle* in part-payment for me taking the Otterton stuff.'

'... which was stolen property you still chose to sell for your own means,' pointed out Jack.

'Finders, keepers, I always thought,' protested Margo. 'It was just my lucky day, wasn't it?'

'Well, we'll see if the day you spend in court turns out just as lucky,' said Bailey, 'because, Margo Berrington, I'm arresting you for theft in that you appropriated property belonging to another with the intention of permanently depriving them of it.'

'What ...?' But that was all Margo had time to say before she and Bryant were being escorted out.

As police car doors slammed, Dexter turned desperately to the DI. 'But

Margo isn't a thief, Inspector. Bryant's the real villain.'

'And for which I'm sure he'll eventually be charged,' assured Bailey, 'assuming your wife is prepared to formally identify him as the man she saw burying the loot.'

'Will that get her off the hook?'

'That remains to be seen, but it might get her a lighter sentence.' Bailey turned to Jack. 'Job done, mate. I'll see you soon for that drink you owe me.'

As the DI made his own exit and the other members sat in disbelief, Jack produced a miniature of brandy and handed it to the ashen-faced Dexter. 'Here, I thought this might be needed.'

'Isn't it just!' Dexter took an immediate swig. 'I knew Margo would have to face the music in the end, but I tried to protect her as long as I could. She wouldn't tell me who it was blackmailing her and even when Bryant didn't pay me for *Pickle*, I didn't cotton on it was him.'

'He was probably leaving it to Margo to explain when the dust had settled,' surmised Jack. 'By then he would doubtless have sold your boat and, together with the other cash Margo had raised, used the proceeds to buy *Osprey*. But, like all blackmailers, it probably wouldn't have stopped there. He had something on you and would have used it ...'

'... until he bled us dry,' accepted Dexter. He shrugged a reluctant acceptance. 'I suppose I should be grateful it's been snipped in the bud. Thanks, Jack. You were only doing your job.'

'Like we all have to do, Dexter. Hopefully, your next one will be a little more fulfilling than the last.' Seeing Laura keen to talk, he made his excuses and went over.

She nodded towards Dexter finishing off his brandy. 'I think we could all do with a stiff one after that session, Jack. For a moment I thought each and every one of us was going to be arrested.'

'Yeah, sorry I put you all through that.'

'I'm just thankful it was Margo who finally got what was coming to her ...' Laura took the glass of wine just handed to her by Charles, '... though I was rather hoping it would be for something rather more serious than handling stolen goods.'

'You mean the murder of your father?' Jack shrugged. 'Give it time, Laura. We're still waiting for some extra toxicology test results, and at least we now have the two of them safely in custody. Doubtless Margo will be only too happy to squeal on Bryant if it means saving her own skin.'

'She'll need a good lawyer,' said Charles.

'Then let's hope she doesn't get one,' snapped back Laura.

Well aware he was scoring no points following that line of thought, Charles merely shrugged and wandered away while Laura turned back to Jack. 'Sorry for that, but he really gets my back up. Anyway, one thing you didn't explain was why Jim's brother Greg also got murdered.'

'There's a lot I didn't explain,' admitted Jack, 'but here and now's probably not the best place and time to do it.'

'Just the same, I'd love to know how you fathomed it all out. Can we meet up somewhere before I leave in a couple of days? In fact, can I have another look at that printout you showed us of Margo's landscape?'

'Sure ... if you tell me what you have in mind?'

'Just this,' she said, pointing to the steam train chugging through the rolling coastal scene. 'Does this line actually exist?'

'It certainly does. That's the North Norfolk Railway, and steam trains run regularly on what was always known as The Poppy Line.'

'Then how about taking a trip on it ourselves ... you and Audrey and me and Mum?' She smiled. 'After all that's happened this past week, it could be just the tonic we need.'

'What about Charles? Would he come as well?'

'I suppose he'd want to.'

'Okay, let's do it then, and the sooner the better if you're all off home soon. How about tomorrow ... eleven o'clock at Sheringham station?'

'Perfect.'

Jack and Audrey said their farewells, leaving the rest of the rally members to come to terms with the bizarre turn events had taken.

'Not the jolliest of get-togethers,' sighed Audrey as they climbed into their car.

'It was never meant to be,' said Jack, starting up and pulling away, 'but perhaps tomorrow will be better.'

'I'm sure we'll have a lovely day,' agreed Audrey after Jack had explained the proposed railway trip. 'That family needs something to cheer it up before they all leave Norfolk.'

'Hmm, maybe,' said Jack, evasively.

'What do you mean?'

'That there's still some tension between Laura and Charles.'

'Oh, Jack, for goodness' sake, stop looking for problems. It's quite natural to have issues between a mother's boyfriend and her daughter. Let's just forget them all, go home and unwind over a cup of tea.'

'Yeah, but I'll just pay another quick visit to Norwich on the way.'

'What for this time?'

'Just a loose end I need to tie up, Aud. It won't take long.'

*   *   *

Chapter Thirteen

'Ah, this is the way to travel,' sighed Audrey, settling back into the carriage's soft upholstery.

'Brings back memories, doesn't it, Aud?' Jack paused to take in the charm of the old-style compartment they'd chosen, with its netted luggage racks, leather-belted window sashes, framed colour prints of holiday destinations and the ever-evocative fragrance of coal smoke and super-heated steam. 'How about you three?'

Seated opposite, Charles merely shrugged, though the two women in his life were clearly enjoying the experience. 'I'm loving it, Jack,' answered Laura, enthusiastically. 'This is the first time I've been on a steam train.'

Helen agreed. 'Such a good idea of yours, Laura. We could be a million miles away, and this fresh sea air will help to blow away all the unpleasantness of yesterday.'

As planned, they had met up on the station platform, Jack delighting in the prospect of another steam experience, and Audrey just glad the recriminations of this rally were finally at an end. And now she too could sit back and enjoy it as, amidst puffs of exhausted steam, the large BR Standard loco with its four carriage load, pulled them smoothly on their way. They were off.

Very soon they were clearing the town and trundling through the slightly undulating countryside, leaving a smoky trail over green woodlands and lush farmland, while catching frequent glimpses between of the cobalt blue expanse of the North Sea.

'How lucky we are to be experiencing this,' said Audrey, as always thinking of others not so blessed. 'I'm sure Margo and Harry's surroundings this morning are anything but pleasant.'

'And serves them right too,' said Laura coldly. 'I just hope they get what they deserve.' She leaned forwards a little towards Jack. 'I hate to spoil this lovely trip, but as Margo's name's been brought up, can you tell me what you meant when you said she owed my father money, and what it was for?'

'I can't be sure myself,' admitted Jack, 'but I think it likely that she simply hadn't handed over receipts from selling recently stolen goods, and then became desperate for even more to pay off Bryant.'

'But, if both she and Bryant were involved in this scam, how come they hadn't met before?' queried Helen.

'Probably just a case of Ralph ensuring that no-one went behind his back to cut him out. Thanks to Margo having no interest in boats or ever attending a *Steambuffs* rally, he could make certain the two didn't even *know* of each other, let alone meet, and that way kept the whole operation in his tight grip.'

Helen gave a heartfelt sigh. 'Ralph really was more devious than we ever realised.'

'And in more ways than one,' agreed Jack. 'Like the way he dealt with Laura's boyfriend.'

Both Helen and Charles flashed looks of annoyance at this betrayal of a confidence, and even Audrey gave her husband a meaningful scowl. Surprised that Jack even knew about her long-lost love, Laura seemed more embarrassed than hurt. 'All in the past, Jack. Okay, it was painful at the time and probably the reason I've avoided men ever since.'

'Except you haven't Laura, have you?'

'What do you mean?'

'I mean you've found yourself a man-friend in Norwich in just this last week.'

She gave a sheepish smile. 'How do you know that?'

'Oh, just little signs,' said Jack, '... that and keeping my eyes open.'

'Laura, is this true?' asked Helen, excited that her daughter might have finally put the past behind her and found some happiness. Beside her, however, Charles looked decidedly uncomfortable and started to fidget in his seat while Laura herself seemed determined to play down this revelation.

'Just someone I met, Mum.'

'Oh, come on, it's a bit more serious than that isn't it, Laura?' persisted Jack, mischievously. 'Right through the rally I think he's been on your mind and I'm sure you're wishing he were here today ... which is why I've arranged a little surprise.'

'You've done *what*?' Laura appeared anything but pleased, Helen and Charles looked bemused and Audrey couldn't believe her husband could be so interfering.

Jack, though, was undeterred. 'I've invited your new boyfriend to join us ... you are pleased, aren't you?'

'I'm not sure ... how did you ...?'

But Laura's questioning was cut short by the train slowing for its first stop at Weybourne. As they pulled into the authentic looking nineteen-fifties station with its hanging baskets of flowers and porters' trolleys laden with travel-stickered luggage, Jack scanned the figures waiting on the platform. Thankfully, the man he was expecting was there and ready to board. A tap on the window showed their location and, by the time they were pulling away for Holt, a good looking chap with the healthy complexion of someone used to fresh air and hard work, was sliding open the compartment door.

As he paused, uncertain of entering, Jack scanned reactions. Judging by their startled looks, Helen and Charles were the most shocked, and Laura seemed far from thrilled. 'Jack, you had no right.'

'Oh, it was no trouble. My treat,' replied Jack, ushering the young man in. 'Well, come on, Laura … aren't you going to introduce us?'

'What? … oh yes … this is Bill Redford, my new boyfriend.'

'Good to finally meet you,' said Jack, tongue-in-cheek, 'even if neither of Laura's introductions are actually true.'

'Jack, what on earth are you talking about?' asked Audrey, confused.

'I'm saying he's neither new, nor Bill Redford.'

'So, who is he then?'

Jack nodded to the stunned couple opposite. 'I think Helen and Charles here can answer that.'

'He's Peter Warmstead,' said Charles, reluctantly.

'Laura's old flame … who … who we all thought died years ago,' stammered Helen.

As Audrey sat open-mouthed, the train's piercing whistle was the only sound to break the stunned silence of that compartment.

*   *   *

'How did you find us out?' asked Peter, taking a seat beside Laura. He had a pleasant voice, deep and resonant and one used to giving instructions.

'By a process of deduction,' said Jack. 'Laura had been frightened by something that morning at the Great Hospital and later, on the Cathedral webcam, I easily spotted her in her yellow sailing coat, going back there. I was intrigued to know why, and even more so next day when she made no mention of it.'

'You could just have minded your own business.' Laura was in no mood for explanations.

'I could,' accepted Jack, 'but then other things started to happen, like Charles' own little fright at the museum when he too caught sight of what he said was a ghost.'

'How did you know that was me?' challenged Peter Warmstead.

'I didn't at the time, and then only recently by watching the TV coverage of the rally. But there you were at the museum, hovering in the background amongst the crowds.'

Laura squeezed her boyfriend's hand. 'I said you were taking a risk coming, Peter.'

'I know, but I just wanted to be near you.' He turned back to Jack. 'But you'd never seen me before, so however did you know who to look for?'

'I had a photo of you,' explained Jack, 'obtained from old newspaper archives and which I cross-checked against the images Laura had taken and emailed to the Master of the Great Hospital. A number of them showed a couple of men working on the very building she'd photographed, and I only needed to enlarge those images to confirm that one of them was you. No wonder Laura collapsed with fright when she zoomed in on a man she'd once loved and thought had died years before.'

Audrey was starting to see the light. 'So he was ...?'

'... one of the builders working there that morning,' confirmed Jack, 'and still is, which is how I lured him onto this train. When we went into Norwich after our get-together yesterday, I popped to the Great Hospital and asked a member of staff to pass on a note telling Peter of our plans and asking him to meet us at Weybourne.'

'I just thought it was an innocent invite,' explained Peter. 'It said not to discuss it with you, Laura, as it was meant to be a surprise.'

'It was certainly *that*,' sighed Laura. 'It's good of you really, Jack, but I just wish you hadn't planned it all behind my back before I'd had a chance to tell Mum.'

'Yes, I was a bit underhand, I'm afraid,' confessed Jack, 'but I was worried about you after your ghostly sighting and couldn't work out what had caused such an alarming reaction. Then Helen told me about your lost love and that he'd been a builder. Putting two and two together, I came to the conclusion that he could possibly be "the friend" you kept going to stay with in Norwich.'

Audrey gave Laura a frown. 'You're very forgiving, my dear. If a serious boyfriend of mine had let me think he'd died in India years before, *I* wouldn't have been so quick to give him a second chance when I found out he hadn't.'

'You would, Audrey, if you knew what had driven him there in the first place.'

'Care to tell us?' invited Jack.

*   *   *

'It's a long story,' said Peter.

'But one I know goes back to when you were refitting Ralph Lampeter's office,' said Jack. 'The way I heard it, you stole some money from his desk.'

'I found *something* in his desk, Jack, but it certainly wasn't money. I was moving it out of the way, when a drawer slid out onto the floor, spilling a whole lot of papers. As I scooped them up and stuffed them back, something caught my eye.'

'Which was ...?'

'... the list of ex-offenders currently being rehabilitated by *New Start*. I suppose I should have minded my own business, but I was interested to read details of their offences, their sentences and release dates. Then I became really intrigued when it also listed their addresses.'

'Addresses?'

'Yeah, except I immediately realised they couldn't possibly live in the posh homes written there, and I was even more suspicious when I saw valuable items listed next to each one. And one of those addresses stood out because I'd worked there myself, repairing damage after a burglary. The owner told me what things had been stolen and they matched those on the list, so it didn't take a brain surgeon to work out ...'

'... that Ralph Lampeter was involved with a crime syndicate systematically robbing big houses,' completed Jack. 'So, what did you do about it?'

'Something pretty daft, in retrospect. I confronted him face to face.'

'That took nerve, Peter.'

'Not really. Laura and I were an item by this time, but her father was dead against me, so I thought if I had something on him, he wouldn't then dare make life difficult for us anymore and I could call the tune.'

'Except it backfired on you?'

Peter nodded, grimly. 'Big time. At first he said it was nothing to do with him and that he'd look into it. But the next day I was called into the office and both him and Seager were there looking really threatening. They said they'd searched my van, found a couple of grand hidden in a side panel and reported it to the police.'

'So, they were framing you?'

'Exactly. I told them I'd let on what I'd really found, but they just laughed and said it would be my word against theirs and they'd make sure the police had all the evidence they needed to charge me.'

'Do we have to listen to this rubbish?' broke in Charles, looking like thunder.

'Why are you getting so agitated if there's no truth in it?' asked Jack. 'I don't think we've heard the half of it, have we, Peter?'

'No, because things got really ugly and they started threatening that if I stayed in the country they had ways of ensuring I'd be out of their hair for good. Then they produced a load of cash and a one-way ticket to India and said I had forty-eight hours to do a disappearing act and that it would be bad news for me if I ever returned.'

'What about Laura?' asked Audrey. 'Didn't you even get to say goodbye and explain what had happened?'

Peter shook his head. 'No chance. They kept tabs on me right until I flew out and then told Laura and her mum the cash-theft story ... and that I'd fled the country for fear of going to court.'

'And, more fool us, we believed them,' said Helen.

'You surely don't believe Warmstead,' protested Charles. 'You know as well as I do the man's a liar as well as a thief.'

'It sounds to me that it's you who's done most of the lying, you bastard,' said Helen, giving her partner a look as barbed as her words. 'As far as I'm concerned, you deserve everything that's coming to you and I never want to clap eyes on you again.' She moved closer to Laura and put a comforting arm around her.

'But we *do* know Peter spent his time in India doing aid work,' defended Audrey.

'And, supposedly getting himself killed in the process,' pointed out Jack. 'Not believing in mortal resurrection, we did contact the aid agencies there who confirmed that two of their Brits really had been caught up in the Jaipur bombings. Peter Warmstead had sadly been killed, but Bill Redford had survived.'

The builder nodded. 'Bill was my best friend out there, Jack. When the bombs went off, I was at the other end of the building they hit. When I made my way back through the wreckage and found his body ...'

'... you saw a heaven-sent opportunity to take on a new identity so it would be safe for you to return to England,' said Jack.

'I know it sounds callous,' admitted Peter, 'but, during our time together, I'd got to know Bill well and that he was an orphan with no family in the UK. In all the confusion, it was easy to just give the authorities *my* name as the one killed, take Bill's passport, get a backstreet scam-artist to change the photo, and use it to come back here and forge a new life.'

'Those bombings made headline news,' said Laura. 'I saw the reports in the papers and was heartbroken when I read you'd been killed. You should've contacted me.'

'I wanted to, but I thought your father and Charles would've convinced you of my guilt, and anyway, I just assumed you'd made another life for yourself and forgotten me. And, as far as I knew, there were still police charges on the books back here.'

'We checked that,' said Jack. 'For obvious reasons, Lampeter and Seager never did really report anything to the police.'

'Perhaps not,' accepted Peter, 'but, with their underworld connections, I knew my life would always be in danger if there was even a hint I was still alive and back in the country. Laura had always told me how she loved Norwich, so I just headed there, lay low, and adopted another life.'

'Until that morning I saw you at the Great Hospital,' said Laura, 'and ...'

'... all your old emotions came flooding back,' completed Audrey with a smile. 'My goodness, if nothing else, this rally has certainly produced some surprises, good and bad, but that must have been quite a shock for you.'

'And for you too, Charles, when you spotted Peter at the museum last Saturday morning,' said Jack. 'No wonder you got straight in touch with your old boss and had him hot-footing it here.'

'I wondered why Ralph had so suddenly changed his mind about attending the rally,' sneered Helen. 'That was you, Seager, you ... you scumbag.'

'But it *has* turned out happily for some,' hastily pointed out Audrey, trying to avoid a full-blown spat. 'At least Laura and Peter have found love again.'

Helen nodded and smiled. 'Yes, that *is* a romantic ending.'

'Except, it isn't the end,' warned Jack. 'You see, Helen, it was your daughter and Peter here who actually murdered your estranged husband.'

'We did *what?*' Laura sat bolt upright in her seat. 'Now you really *have* gone too far, Jack. You know as well as I do that it was Margo who murdered my father.'

'That's right, Jack, by spiking his drink,' added Helen. 'Margo must have known about Ralph's heart condition, and I'm sure it wasn't difficult for her to steal some of his *digitalis* and simply add it to his whisky that night.'

'That's certainly what we were meant to believe, but Margo didn't kill anyone.' Jack nodded towards the love birds, sitting opposite, holding hands rather tighter than before but, nevertheless, doing their best to look affronted. 'I can understand how you two felt with all those wasted years apart, but it doesn't justify taking a life and putting the blame on a woman you hated.'

'Who said I did?' Laura gave a little laugh. 'That's a good story, Jack, but you are forgetting one important fact ... that Peter and I were in Norwich when my father died and we have plenty of witnesses to prove it.'

'And *we* have proof you *did*, Laura. It was deviously cunning and brilliantly effective, but DI Bailey rang me last night with the latest toxicology results, which showed us how.'

The train was slowing again as they neared Holt. Jack stood up and put a hand on the young couple's shoulders. 'Time to go, you two. It's the end of the line, I'm afraid ...' gliding into the station, he could see several uniformed police and DI Bailey waiting on the platform, '... in more ways than one.'

*　　*　　*

Epilogue

'This must be where *Telegraph* sailed from,' pointed out Jack, as he and Audrey looked down from Norwich's Foundry Bridge to the slack waters of the River Wensum below. Just a little further on, with wisps of smoke curling upwards from her funnel, *Osprey* lay awaiting her first passengers. It was a lovely summer's afternoon and ideal for the short trip downriver to Brundall. 'I wonder what the weather was like on that fateful day?'

'If it was a Good Friday, probably a lot cooler,' said Audrey as they made their way down to the quay, 'but I guess now we'll never find out by reading that article Laura was going to write on the disaster.' She gave a heartfelt sigh. 'To think, a couple of months ago you were all looking forward to the rally. Now *Steambuffs* has been wound up with one of its members dead, three in custody and another pending charges.'

'But here's one who did come through it all okay,' said Jack, brightening, as Dexter jumped ashore to greet them.

'Good to see you both.' His broad smile reinforced the words.

'Thanks for inviting us, Dexter. Are we really your first passengers?'

'You and a few others. This will just be a shakedown trip before we start regular services.' He turned back to *Osprey*, her paintwork shining and brass fittings glinting in the sunlight. 'Come on, let's get you both a drink.'

'"Shipshape and Bristol fashion",' quoted Jack admiringly as they stepped aboard. 'You've done a great job with her, Dexter.'

'Not just me, Jack.' A smiling figure in a white boiler suit was just emerging from the engine-room hatch. 'Our engineer here has worked his old magic.'

'And loved every minute of it,' said Jim Rowston, characteristically wiping his hands on a piece of cotton waste, 'thanks to you, Jack.'

'Just glad things have turned out well for you, Jim.'

'Better than I could have wished.' He turned to Dexter. 'Steam's up and engine ready when you are, Skipper.'

'Great. We'll get under way in about fifteen minutes.'

'There's a man happy in his work,' said Jack as the engineer went back to his world of gleaming machinery and super-heated steam. 'I'm sure staying busy takes his mind off losing his brother so tragically.'

'Indeed, and I hear Greg's inquest has been adjourned until after Margo's trial.'

'Which comes up soon,' recalled Jack. 'How is she dealing with that prospect?'

'Intolerantly, like Margo handles most things, though hoping for a lenient sentence by giving evidence against Bryant.'

'It must be difficult for you having her at home on bail,' sympathised Audrey.

'It's purgatory, but not for much longer.' Dexter shrugged broad shoulders. 'I've accepted reality and am filing for divorce.'

'A wise move ...' Jack nodded towards the saloon, '... but enough of that. I think we could all do with that drink you promised.'

'Absolutely, and come and meet the cabin crew.'

The identity of the stewardess handing them glasses of champagne as they entered was indeed a surprise. 'Helen!'

She smiled. 'Don't look so shocked. It's about time I earned a living.' In uniform white shirt and black slacks, she looked younger than ever and amazingly unscarred by events. 'I'm actually looking forward to seeing passengers enjoying my old boat.'

'*Our* old boat,' corrected Dexter. 'We're business partners now, remember.' He turned to Jack and Audrey. 'In the end, Lionel bought *Pickle*, so I used that money to buy a half-share in *Osprey*, which Helen and I are now going to operate together.'

'With me as the trolley-dolly,' laughed Helen. 'It'll be fun.'

Audrey frowned over her champagne glass. 'How does your Charles feel about that?'

'I don't know and, frankly, I don't care because he's not *my* Charles anymore. If Ralph did me one favour, Audrey, it was holding out against giving me a divorce. Thank goodness he did and I never married that louse of a lawyer.' Helen allowed herself just a little smile of satisfaction. 'Mind you, he's going to need all his legal skills soon, because the police have called him in for a chat about *his* involvement in *New Start*.'

'That charity was a dirty business all round,' said Jack. 'I just hope Peter and Laura will get lighter sentences once the full facts are known.'

'Fingers crossed.' Helen made an effort to brighten. 'But life goes on and, right now, we have a boat to run and passengers to look after.'

'And here they are,' said Dexter as voices sounded at the afterdeck. 'You already know them so let's go up.'

'It's the Hillbecks and Edwards!' exclaimed Audrey as she recognised the other guests filing aboard. 'How wonderful to see them again.'

'And in more pleasant circumstances than last time,' said Dexter. 'Right, if you chaps look after the lines, we'll get going.'

With mooring ropes slipped and hauled aboard, a toot on the steam whistle and a jangle of telegraph bells, they were off. As other Norwich bridges passed overhead and riverside buildings and developments, new and old, glided quietly by on either side, Audrey sighed. 'What a perfect way to spend an afternoon, Jack. Laura would love this, wouldn't she?'

Over-hearing the remark, Pat Hillbeck sidled over. 'She had her chance, Audrey, and it's Helen I feel sorry for now. She's told us the whole sorry tale and what a low-life that Ralph turned out to be, ruining so many lives.'

'Including hers,' added Eileen Edwards, joining them at the rail. 'Let's face it, poor Helen's lost her husband, daughter and partner in one fell swoop ...' she nodded in the direction of the saloon, '... which is why I think it would be good if us girls went and kept her company and leave these lads to do their boaty thing up here.'

'Good idea.'

As the three wives disappeared below, Lionel and Doctor Edwards emerged, the latter armed with two large glasses of lager, one of which he handed to Jack. 'Thought this might be more up your street than champers.' Already the steady thump of *Osprey*'s engine was bringing them into semi-rural surroundings and another waterway feeding in on their starboard side. 'The River Yare already.' He waved his glass casually towards wooded banks now starting to line the waterway. 'Amazing how quickly the scene changes.'

Jack nodded. 'Like life, John. It seems no time at all that we first met on the rally.'

'And yet so much has happened since,' added Lionel. 'What a rotten business that was.'

'For all of us,' agreed Jack. 'Bryant and Margo got what was coming to them, so no sympathy there, but I can't help feeling sorry for Laura. She worked hard to make the rally a success and, as we know, it turned out to be anything but. In a way, I think we can all understand her and Peter doing what they did.'

'Definitely,' agreed Doctor Edwards, 'but it still doesn't explain the mystery of the whole thing. They had witnesses who swear they were in Norwich when Lampeter's murder took place, so how on earth did they do it?'

'Very cleverly,' said Jack. He cocked an ear towards the saloon and the voices of their wives happily chatting. 'Let's go for'ard and I'll tell you.'

From the wheelhouse came another jangle of the telegraph as *Osprey* cleared the city limits and Dexter rang down for an increase in speed.

*   *   *

'They say "old sins cast long shadows",' quoted Jack, 'and they certainly did in this case. As Helen has already explained to you, Laura had plenty of reasons for hating her father, but it was only when Peter told her of the true purpose of *New Start* and how he'd been set up and threatened, that she wanted him dead. Laura and Peter were still besotted with each other and wanted nothing more than to be together, but they knew his life would always be in danger as long as her father was alive. Things came to a head quickly though when Charles spotted Peter in the museum and alerted Ralph, who hot-footed it here to join the rally. Laura knew that to protect Peter, they had to act quickly so, to that end, they hatched the perfect murder.'

'Yes, but *how?*' urged Doctor Edwards.

'It had me puzzled for a while,' admitted Jack, 'until the night I was complaining to Audrey of all the things you have to do before actually getting into bed at night. You tell me, John ... what's the most basic?'

'Cleaning our teeth?'

'Exactly, and something Laura knew her fastidious father would never neglect, even on his boat.'

'You mean it was *his toothpaste* that was poisoned?'

'Exactly. Dexter told me he'd heard someone drive in to Sutton Staithe and go to *Osprey* sometime around midnight after the dinner on Saturday. I thought at the time it might have been Jim returning from Yarmouth, though Dexter said it was a while before the car drove away. I'm sure now that it was Peter bringing Laura the poison to inject straight into Ralph's tube of toothpaste ready for when he stayed aboard *Osprey* the following night.'

'Ingenious, but the autopsy only showed normal levels of *digitalis* in his body, Jack, so how did it kill him?'

'It didn't. It was something far more deadly and, once again, I have to thank my dear wife for putting me on the right trail.'

'Audrey?'

'Yes. We were at Sutton Staithe a few days after the murder, testing another theory I had, and while there she commented on how we didn't eat out very often. An innocent remark, but one that reminded me that Laura had said they had supper at an Indian restaurant the night of the murder. Now, only the day before, Helen had told me how Peter had gone to India when he skipped the country. Not a particularly significant connection, I grant you, but then Audrey also mentioned the oak tree at How Hill, presented at the thirty-six

Berlin Olympics?'

'I know that tree,' said Lionel. 'It's just a stump now, but what's that got to do with anything?'

'Just that Audrey remarked how even trees could sometimes have sinister associations. I put that together with the Indian connection and recalled an article I'd read months before. It was about the *Cerbera odollam* tree.'

'*Cerbera* ... what?' asked Doctor Edwards.

'*Odollam*, but called the Pong-Pong tree in India where it grows. But don't let that light-hearted name fool you. It's also called "The Murder Tree", and for good reason, because its seeds contain *cerberin*, which screw up the heart's electrical system and stop it dead in short order. No-one knows how many people a year die from it, either by accident, murder or suicide, because it's undetectable unless a toxicologist knows what he's looking for, and virtually unheard of in this country.'

'... until it was found in Lampeter?'

'Yes, but only after they conducted very specialised tests.'

'But you don't swallow toothpaste, Jack,' reasoned Lionel, 'so how come it poisoned him?'

'Because *cerberin* is so deadly, it only has to be absorbed through the skin to be fatal.'

'And, remember, Ralph already had a cardiac problem anyway,' pointed out Doctor Edwards, 'so it probably didn't take much to kill him.' He frowned. 'But, from what I gather, Seager must have been party to all Lampeter's threats and deception. Surely they would have had to bump him off as well.'

'No, they knew they were safe there,' said Jack. 'With Ralph dead, Seager would have been terrified his own involvement in the *New Start* scam would come out. He had no links to the underworld and, anyway, would have been answerable to Helen who liked Peter and would never have allowed Charles to ruin her daughter's life again.'

'But, Jim Rowston's brother was killed,' said Lionel. 'Why was that?'

'Ah yes, poor Greg,' said Jack, shaking his head sadly. 'That was one factor they never reckoned on. He'd been sleeping rough with not even bare essentials. I checked his rucksack myself and there was no toothpaste in there. So, when Jim brought him on board *Osprey* and put him in the late Ralph's cabin for the night, he must've helped himself to the toiletries left there.'

'So, did they find this *cerberin* toxin in him as well?' asked Doctor Edwards.

'They did. It really is deadly stuff, and Peter has already admitted he brought it back from India as a form of insurance in case Lampeter's bully boys ever caught up with him.'

'But, in the end, used it to extract revenge on the very man responsible.

Poetic justice, I suppose,' mused Doctor Edwards, 'and very clever because, at the time, we were all so sure Margo had done it. I saw her myself, driving away the night of the murder.'

'And they found her prints on that wine glass in the saloon,' added Lionel, 'which proved she'd been there longer than the few minutes she claimed.'

'Ah yes, that wine glass,' recalled Jack. 'Do you remember, John, on the morning of the murder I said there was something missing that should have been there ... the coffee pot ... but something there that shouldn't be. I was referring to that wine glass which seemed very ordinary and didn't match the cut-glass ones hanging behind *Osprey*'s bar. When I took Audrey back to Sutton Staithe, I noticed it was identical to the wine glasses used there. Now, on the night of our dinner, I'd heard Laura's bag clanking as we came out. She laughed it off as half-drunk bottles of wine, but now I was sure it was something else. I checked the bill for that night and, sure enough, our normally honest Laura had paid for one broken glass. But it hadn't been broken ...'

'... she'd taken Margo's glass from the table with her fingerprints on it,' figured out Lionel.

'... in order to frame her for the murder she was planning the following night,' completed Doctor Edwards. 'But how about Lampeter's tumbler of whisky though? That *was* found laced with *digitalis*.'

'Yes, and probably staged by Laura in the minutes before she raised the alarm,' explained Jack. 'It would have been easy to quickly pour a shot and then add a few drops of her father's medication to further throw the blame.'

Lionel shook his head. 'Fiendishly simple.'

'But enough to lay the blame firmly on Margo's head. Revenge indeed ...' Jack sighed, '... if it had come off, that is.'

'But a bit extreme, even for Margo,' grinned Lionel. He nodded aft to the wheelhouse and Dexter contentedly helming them down the river. 'Either way, though, he's seen the light and will be best rid of her.'

'Amen to that,' said Doctor Edwards.

'Who's that being all biblical?' asked Audrey with a smile as she joined them on the foredeck. 'The only prayer I'm making right now is that we forget murder and mayhem for the next hour or so and enjoy the rest of this trip.' She nodded in the direction of the saloon. 'Helen's just made some tea if you're ready.'

'Well, I am for one,' said Doctor Edwards. 'Come on, Lionel, let's go see what goodies those lovely wives of ours have got to tempt us with.'

'Aren't you coming, Jack?' Audrey wasn't used to her husband holding back if cakes and a cuppa were on offer.

'In a minute, Aud.' He was leaning over the for'ard rail, watching *Osprey*'s

150

lean bow cleaving the Yare's wide waters, yet leaving only the most modest of wakes. 'Just enjoying a bit more steam propulsion while I can.'

'Why not.' Audrey joined him at the rail. 'Strange how this whole saga started with a trip on a steamboat and now it's ending with one.'

'So it is,' acknowledged Jack, putting an arm around his wife. 'Perhaps a sign of putting the past behind and accepting the future.'

'At least we've got one.' Audrey gave a little shiver. 'It's just starting to get cool. Are you ready for that tea now?'

'You bet I am.'

'And while we're down there, Jack, you can also get me a miniature of brandy.'

Her husband looked concerned. 'Not *that* cold, are you?'

'No, it's not for now, Jack. I want to use it for cleaning my teeth tonight.' She gave him a dig and a smile. 'You just don't know what might be in the toothpaste.'

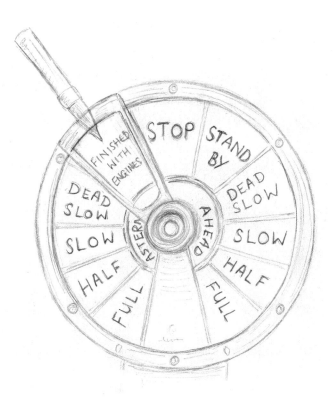

Dear Reader

Thanks so much for buying this latest "Jack Fellows" story. I hope you enjoyed it. If you did, but there are others in the series you haven't yet read, all the books shown on the inside front cover are available through my website:
www.chriscrowther.co.uk

*Each costs only £6.95 plus a **per order** charge of £2.00 for post & packing, so a multiple order does bring the unit cost down.*

One extra book you may want to order is TIMECRUISER, my children's book shown on the inside cover opposite. A fantasy adventure, it encompasses significant events in Broadland history and is a fun read, while at the same time giving the background to this magical bit of the kingdom. Aimed at 8 – 12 year-olds, it seems to have been enjoyed just as much by grown-ups, so don't be shy at ordering that one as well. Price for TIMECRUISER is just £4.95.

Many thanks again for all your interest in my books and looking forward very much to hearing from you.

Best wishes and happy reading.

Chris